Frederick Tuccat Gray aka Cory Bluestone

STONES
ON
A HOPELESS
ISLAND

STONES ON A HOPELESS ISLAND

Cast of Characters

Corin: A young man who is still trying to figure out life with a big heart and sometimes has "moments" that make you wonder.

Kikai: A loving, kind, blue-haired woman who takes care of both the Sandlands village and Corin.

Seena: Strong minded and a great fighter. She carries herself with a serious mindset and appearance that shows more than her softer side from time to time.

Nikai: Praised as a good leader with good morals by her people. Her green hair matches the same exact colors of the green fields and trees.

Lawowl: One of the oldest and wisest people on the island. Loyal to the people and island, he will do whatever it takes to protect home.

To my reader and my intended audience:

My name is Frederick Tuccat Gray but I'd much rather preferred to be called by my nickname that I grew up with "Cory". I'm currently becoming an English Major through community college. I want to say thank you so much for taking your time to read my first ever written short story that I hope to evolve into more in the future. It's been a five-year journey of this book finally happening. When I first announced I was going to take a shot at making book after the six plus years of journal writing with friends and family, I was surprised by the lack of encouraging support. I feel into depression that nearly destroyed me and my confidence. I needed a chance. A chance to bounce back and prove it to myself that I can still make things happen even after a couple of bad things happening. All it took was a conversation and one special day to help me get back on track in making this story. I confessed to my co-worker how much I hated feeling like shit and that I can't seem to let go of my hurtful past. She told me I needed to let it go. The next day I served a passenger with a big bag of stones. We had a cool conversation about life and then he left to his flight. He came back minutes later to hand me a beautiful blue stone. Told me it belonged to me and it would balance out my life with positive energy. I lost that blue stone three times and all three times it came back to me. It was faith and it was exactly what I needed to make this happen.

The fictional story that I present to you is one about taking a chance and giving yourself a chance. Just how I took a chance in accepting that bluestone from a stranger. I believe we live in a world that believes in "invisible books and rules". Such as you are limited to what you can be. Being only what society deems fit for you that is acceptable. My main character Corin is someone that sees this on Hope island. He is bothered by the feeling of being "Stuck". Stuck is that feeling that comes to a go-getter when they are annoyed at a not so likeable job just to keep getting by knowing there is something better. Corin believes there is more to life that just feeding a village. Especially since he is coming to the classic age of twenty-one in wanting to figure out what to do with rest of his life. It requires taking a risk. This four-lettered word can sound terrifying to people who want to play it safe in life. Corin has the pleasure of meeting the rest of the cast exploring the idea of risk in situations of pressure against their personalities. The personalities I'm referring to are the ones that don't see themselves accountable of guilt. Instead they hold on to the past that affects the present. Specially, a past event called the Great Betrayal that occurred when he was only a baby. An event that plays a factor into Corin's adventure as he deals with being annoyed by it. Little does he know both figuratively and literally, there are others in that are trying to deal with the ways of living on this once Hopeful Island. His desire to see more past the gates around his village and the affect of the Great Betrayal on the island lead into a much bigger universe neither him nor the others could ever imagine.

Prologue

A grumpy elderly man wearing brown farmer clothes, comes out of his cabin with a fishing stick. He gazes upon the morning sun shining upon his cabin and the lake in front of him. "Too damn bright, eh. But it's a beautiful day to fish." He walks over to a pile of rocks near a lake. A grand smile appears on his face as he walks towards his favorite spot near the lake. He lunges the string into the water and sits on the rocks. "Nothing beats peace and quiet".

He turns and sees his wife in a glowing green dress comes out of the cabin yelling. "Stone! Make sure to catch a bunch of fish! We need food to last us for days honey." She walks back inside muttering "Love him but he can be a real stubborn MAN!

Stone laughs at her comment. "I will once you be quiet! You'll scare all the fish away Mira!" She walks back into the cabin. Stone sets his eyes on the water. He feels a tug on the line and pulls with all of his strength. A large fish emerged! "Wow! Easily, this will last us a week alone. We are going to eat good tonight." Stone put the fish on the ground and carefully pulled out a knife to kill the fish. He noticed blood dripping from the fish. "Was this fish in a fight?" He walked back over to the lake and gazed at the water. A streaking set of red lines appeared in the water. Stone was startled at the discovery of blood in the lake. "This came upstream. What is going on?" Stone ran up the hill following the stream from the lake towards the large waterfall. Stone gasped for air. "It's been years since I've ran that hard!" Stone wiped the sweat off his face and sees someone lying unconscious near the waterfall. "Hey!" Stone runs to the sight of a bloodied beaten boy. He examines the boy and checks for a pulse. "He's still breathing! I'm getting you out of here." Stone takes off his shirt and covers up the boys wounded backside. He picks him up and carries him down the hill to his cabin. Stone proceeds to kick the door open and lays him on the floor. "Mira!" he yells. "Get some blankets, cloths, and hot water!" Mira comes out of the room with the items and gasps.

"What happened Stone? Is he alright?" She runs by his side and leans on his large arms. "Can you hear me?" Stone said. She gets to work immediately on his wounds. She lays covers on the floor as Stone places him on top. She places her hands on the side of his head. Her hands begin to light up bright blue and green. "Oh, my it's been years since I've done this." The lights begin to travel around his body for a few seconds until they have vanished. Coughs begin to occur from the boy. "He is alive!"

The young boy awakens. "Where am I?"

"My name is Stone. I'm a fisherman. I found you near the waterfalls unconscious and injured. Luckily for you, we have just enough to bandage you up." Mr. Stone gives a wink to Mira. He begins to grab chairs for all three of them and assists the boy on his feet. He points at the chair facing the two chairs Mira and Stone sit. "Now that I've shared who I am, it is your turn. Who are you and what brings a young boy like yourself this far out on hope island? Mr. Stone waits patiently with his arms crossed and head tilted.

The young man can barely make eye contact. He looks down at his hands and glances at both of them eagerly waiting for his response. "Well, my name is Corin and I came from the Sandlands village."

Mr. Stone quickly responds "The Sandlands? Corin, you aware that all of our villages have an arrangement to not trespass? Also, how are you from the Sandlands but you wear clothing from the Natura village?

Corin nodded "It's a long story Mr. Stone. I'll try to explain as best I can." He stands up and speaks terrified. "I had no choice but to leave. Invaders came to my home and I was forced to find help."

Mr. Stone then jumps out of his chair and become furious with Corin's response. Mira quickly grabbed his fist. "Let him explain." Stone sighed and unclenched his fist. "Now, it's okay Corin. My name is Mira. I'm his wife. You are safe now. Please continue."

Corin begins to slowly shed tears as he speaks. "It was horrible. My friends, my family. I do not know if everyone is alive.

Mira listened attentively as he spoke. Stone turns to Mira and replies "Did you noticed the blue stone in his bag? We have not seen this since…. We last spoke to her.

Mira walks over to Corin and puts her hands on his shoulders "I noticed a stab wound on your right side and a very blue beautiful stone in your bag."

"Where did you get that Corin?" said Mr. Stone. "Be sure to explain this very carefully. Really think this one out."

Corin replies "My caretaker Kikai gave it to me."

Mira and Stone looked at each other in shock. Mira walked over to Mr. Stone and hugged him very tightly. The two begin to whisper. "He's an angel. Is it possible that Corin is…??"

Stone stopped Mira abruptly "Wait. I know where you are going with this Mira. First, we need to know how in the world he got here. Then will share our true thoughts. Mira nodded and Stone spoke aloud to Corin. "Okay Corin, we are ready to hear it. Mira and Mr. Stone both sat eagerly in front of Corin just hoping their thoughts are positive.

Corin speaks in his head "I really hope these two can help me find my way back. Okay, I'll take it one breathed, one sentence, one word at a time." He walks over and picks up the blue stone. "Well it was only a few days ago…"

Chapter One: The Curiosity of Corin

It was a sunny bright late afternoon. The waves near the shore of the Sandlands village were calm and the birds flying by in the sky heading home to their nest. The wind blows into a large field full of crops and into the direction of Corin's face. He feels the dirt coming into his hair and his eyes. "Damn! I wish it the wind could stop." He walks the fields double checking all the crops. Making sure every plant has been watered and every row is complete. The wind continues to blow harder. Water from the sea suddenly rises. A small wave of it is being summoned by his secretive but magical caretaker Kikai. She chuckles at the thought of seeing his brown clothing getting soaked. Her hair and eyes light up blue like the ocean. She lunges her hand towards Corin. The water lands on him and he begins to whine. "No! I just dried these. I want this day to be over with already." Kikai laughs hysterically under her breathe. Once she had her moment of laughter, she called upon Corin to come back to her home.

 Corin! Corin!" Lady Kikai yells "Come inside Corin. Her knees felt the chills of the winds as she wore her favorite light brown dress. Her bright black and blue hair makes her an impossible sight for Corin to miss. "Don't worry about those crops. Will do it tomorrow. Tonight, we celebrate young man!"

Corin puts the equipment onto a wheel barrel. He wipes the sweat off his forehead. He pulls his hair back and ties it into a bun.

Admiring his work, He begins to speak to himself. "I can't wait to get some food! Work has been killing me all day. No more random weather." He yells back at Kikai "I'm on my way Kikai." He runs to through the now wet dirt field seeing mud all over his shoes. "Definitely taking these off before I go inside. She will easily scream at me." He takes of his shoes and puts it next to the front door. Kikai greets Corin as she awaits him at the door. "Short today? This is new. I could get use to this." Corin scratches his head as she goes into her quarters humming. Large noises of items dropping has Corin curious. "You okay Kikai?"

She tells Corin "Close your eyes and you'll find out. Give me just a minute." Corin takes a seat at the table and waits anxiously. BOOM! A loud sound comes from Kikai's room. "I'm coming!" Her door swings open and sings to Corin "Happy birthday!"

"Oh, my goodness! You remembered." Corin smiles with joy as Kikai brings food and a leaf wrapped gift. "Wow, Kikai thank you so much for doing this." He gives her a hug. "Twenty-one years went by so fast." He gazes at the gift in his hand. "What is this? It's heavy! I will open it once we eat. I'm starving."

Kikai kisses him on the cheek as they both sit down to eat. "It's been a long time since we have celebrated your birthday, so I figured maybe this is the time to end that terrible streak. Twenty-one to be exact. You deserve this. The work you've for me. Nobody else is willing to do this except you. Thank you."

Corin chuckles at the gesture. "I mean, this is all I know how to do. I have no friends and family so this is all I have.

Kikai puts her spoon down and finishes chewing. She wipes her face and drinks some water. She takes a moment to look at him chewing. Her stare eventually was captured as he sees she is silent. "Am I not your family? I've raised you since you were a small baby." She stares heavily at him in disappointment as he realizes the mistake in his words. "Don't think I'm so old lady without feelings. If you only knew how hard it is to…"

"I'm sorry. You are right" said Corin. He reaches and holds her hand. "Please forgive my foolish ranting. It's been a long day and I should be more grateful to you. For everything." He leans over to her and kisses her cheek.

She smiles at Corin's sweet apology. She sighs "You are special. Different, but special. You have always had a family. There's me and your Uncle Brutus." She sees outside her window into the now night sky a shooting star. She gasp and turns to him "Make a wish." He closes his eyes and holds his hand tightly. He mutters a long quiet wish with his mouth moving well over a minute.

"Can I tell you what I wish for?" said Corin. He opens his eyes, takes a deep-breathe and holds his hands nervously. She anxiously wonders what he wished for. "I need to explore the rest of the island Kikai. I know what you are going to say but I still want to. Seriously, I am not a kid anymore. It's time"

Kikai becomes insecure and defensive. She grabs her hair and yells "NO! NO! NO! This can't happen Corin. The island has been divided between the villages because of the Great Betrayal. That stupid war. I don't want you to get in trouble."

He gets up out of his chair out of frustration. His places his hands on the table and rolls his eyes. "Do you ever get tired of saying that? I have heard this a thousand times. That happened a long time ago before I was even born. Why does this have to affect what I want to do with my life? Can't just be here forever Kikai. Don't you ever want to do more than just be here and feeding the village?"

She rolls her eyes back at him and places her hands on his shoulders. As soon as Kikai was about to further explain a loud thunder and hail is heard outside. "You should head home now. Don't worry I'll clean this up." Corin gets up and heads towards the door. He opens the door and pauses. Turns at the sight of Kikai slowly cleaning up the table.

"Kikai?" said Corin.

She looks up at him. He wipes the tears off her face. "Corin, I hate the island rules too. I pray this will all end one day and go back to when it was most beautiful." The two have share one last hug as he heads off home. Kikai noticed an object on the table. "Damn it, he forgot the gift." She walks into her bedroom and sits on top of the bed looking at the ceiling. She starts to mutter "At some point, he's going to have to know the truth. I'm trying my best sister."

Corin angrily walks towards the hill to get home. He then starts talking to himself. "I hate this place. So sick and tired of the same thing every day. Clean, harvest, cook, and get a bunch of crap from the other villagers." He sees the ungrateful villagers standing outside their cabins preparing to do their usual taunting. Their eyes on Corin are filled with hateful emotions towards a hideous sight.

"Hey, Are you crazy?" An elderly lady screamed.

"Nope he's not crazy, he's retarded." The elderly man and woman walk back inside his cabin. Corin walks with his head down in shock of the loud negative comments. Suddenly he bumps right into a tall man and his group.

"Hey look! It's the guy who doesn't know how to cook!" said Mikken. Him and his large group laughed hysterically at Corin. "I'm starving. Get back to work and bring me some bread."

Corin clenched his teeth for a moment. His jaw then loosened. He decided to mock Mikken. "Not in the mood for your antics Mikke. How about tomorrow like everyone else? Or better yet." Corin puts his finger in his face. "You must have forgotten that the bread your looking for is right up your ass!"

The whole group behind Mikken began to laugh at him instead. "Wow, this explains why there's not enough to go around!"

Corin continues on. "You seemed pretty happy eating the fish I cooked. You must have eaten the fish's bones too. Explains why your too slow and stupid to Oh!"

Bothered by his words, he clenches his fist and swings right at Corin's gut. The impact of Mikken's punch sends him on his kness. Mikken towers over Corin and grabs him by the hair. "I've got better things to do like make sure pieces of crap don't get out of line!" The group watches Mikken pummel Corin to the ground.

Some cheer while others asked him to stop. "C'mon Mikke this isn't funny anymore." Corin's vision becomes a blurry by each punch being thrown at him. As he puts his hands up for cover, he no longer hears fist being landed at him.

He sees a large man of authority holding Mikken by the neck along with his group being sent away from the scene. "Break it up! Break it up!" said Jo. He instructs his fellow guards to make them leave. He punches Mikken in the gut and puts him in an arm lock. "There's one man in this village in charge and it's not you."

"Dad! Let go of me now!" Mikken cries in pain. "We were just messing around, right Corin?" His dad squints at Corin's face. Seeing bruises on his face, arms, and little blood in the nose.

The dad becomes fed up and annoyed by his son's remarks. "I'm old, but not that old. Say you are sorry. NOW."

Mikken gulps and looks towards Corin. "SSSSoooorrryy Corin."

Jo strengthens his grip. "LOUDER! With genuine feeling to it!"

Mikken gulps "Corin, I apologize for my actions. It won't happen again." Mikken falls flat to the ground.

"Get home now. We are going to talk about this later." Jo helps Corin up to his feet. "You okay?"

Corin sadly nods at him. "Sir, can I go home now? My house is right up that hill near the cliff."

"In a minute. I got some cloths and hot water near the gate. Follow me."

Jo leads the way and He introduces Corin to the village doctor. The doctor takes Corin in. After a short time, the doctor spoke. "Corin, your good to go but you can't work tomorrow. Just rest."

Corin gasps "I thought you said I was good. Kikai is going to need my help tomorrow for food for everyone."

The doctor snickers and looks at the guards waiting outside. "I understand your concern. So, an arrangement was made. Those villagers and specifically Mikken's friends, will personally make sure Kikai has help." The doctor walks Corin out of the cabin.

Jo approaches Corin and lightens up the mood. "Hey Kid, looking good! Enjoy your day off. Mikken will work in your place." He extends his hand out to him. "By the way kid, my name is Jo. Your Corin right?" The two shake hands. "Kikai always says the nicest things about you. Between you and me, you've got what I called the stuff."

Corin tilts his head at Jo. "What does that mean?"

"It means you got the guts to feed the village. Being the only helper for Kikai means your good in my book Corin. Go get some rest Corin. I believe that fellow with the cane is waiting for you over there." Despite the praise he received from Jo, he still feels the hurt on Kikai's face from earlier.

"Thank you for your help Jo" said Corin.

Corin feels a huge sense of relief at the sight of Uncle Brutus waving at him. "I was getting worried sick Corin. Got some food waiting for you at home."

"I can go for some food right about now." Once they both made it up hill and into the home, Uncle Brutus stomped his feet in anger. He sees the blankets hanging out on the line were soaking wet. "Damn it! I forgot to grab our blankets outside before it hailed. Can you bring those in for me while I start a fire to warm up the cabin?"

Corin replies "No problem Uncle." He heads outside and begins to collect the blankets hanging on a clothing line. Footsteps approached him from behind. "Uncle, go back inside I've got this." He turns around and sees the sight of a tall dark figure. He immediately falls on his back screaming. "Don't kill me!" He closes his eyes trembling in fear. After a minute of waiting, the stranger offered a hand to Corin once he opens his eyes.

"I'm not here to kill you. Not yet. Just here to talk." Corin brushes the dirt off his clothes and replies "Why is your face hidden by that dark cloth? Who are you?

The stranger replies "It's not about who am I. It's who are you?" Corin becomes frozen by his dark chilling voice. "The Great Change will be coming soon. Be prepared." The stranger then disappears out of thin air.

"How? What's going on?" Corin then turns to the cabin as Brutus calls for him.

"Come in, Corin the food is ready!" He then slowly looks around, picks up the blankets, and walks back to the cabin unsure of how to feel about the situation. Brutus points at Corin's plate. "Here's that salmon and bread combination you love so much!"

Corin turns to Brutus. "Uncle, may I eat this tomorrow? I'm real tired." Brutus's face was shocked by his response. He thought to himself "Corin loves to eat. I have never seen him turn down food. Especially Salmon." Brutus answers Corin's question "Yes, of course."

Corin walks into his room and closes the door. He lays in bed and stares at the ceiling. "Great Change? I wonder what that means?" He grabs his blanket and turns over with closed eyes. "Finally, I get to sleep."

From a distance, the stranger stands near the edge of the hill that Corin and Brutus resides. He looks upon the village with a sinister smile. "Our master's plan will work perfectly." He turns to his left and speaks to his fellow hooded partner looking at the stars. "What's going Kustar?" he said.

"Was that necessary?" said Kustar. "We were told to find him and watch him. Not threaten him Mustar." Kustar looks up to the sky. "I want the same thing you want. Our families back. But not like that."

Mustar laughs at Kustar's remarks. He pushes his fiercely. "You are as soft as the night's winds! I'm doing what I have been told. I could care less about his feelings or yours. Are you with me?" Kustar grows quiet. His face draws concern as his friends remarks only thickens the moment. "I asked you a question. Give me an answer." He speaks slowly and tauntingly. "Are.You.With.Me?"

Kustar reaches into his pocket and pulls out a small piece of clothing that fits the size of a child. He grasps it tightly with emotion and disbelief. "Yes, I'm with you."

Chapter 2 The Awakening

Corin and Brutus walk together towards the docks east of the village. As they make their way to the docks, both them sit on crates as they wait for Brutus's boat to be ready. "Five minutes sir!" The dockman yells.

"For the thousandth time, you said you saw a ghost?" Brutus chuckles at his face. "I mean are you sure? Sounds like to me you work so much out in that field you probably forgot to take a break. Those exist you know."

Corin grabs Brutus by the arm. His eyes sparked frustrated rage. "This isn't funny Brutus. Listen, I had a long day yes and there are times I don't take a break. You have to understand I wouldn't lie. I'm a terrible liar!" He lets go of his arm.

Brutus then grabs Corin by his arm. "Calm down. I know you are not a liar. It's just I… I haven't heard of anything like that since…

Corin tilts his head. He sees Brutus quietly calms down and enters deep thought gazing into the ocean. "Are you ok Uncle Brutus?" Brutus replies "Yes, Corin I am. It's just I haven't heard anything like that since your father."

"Really?" said Corin.

He shakes his head "Yeah, he just would tell me things like this all the time before he passed." He takes a moment to recollect himself as he looks towards the sun.

"It would be nice if you finally told me more about my family" said Corin. "Why is it so difficult to share these things with me?"

The dock man yells "It's time. The boat is ready."

Brutus replies "I will tell you more when the time is right. I'll be back in a few days."

 The two say their farewell as Brutus enters the boat. He waves him off and walks back to the trail heading toward the village. He begins to speak to himself outloud. "Geerrrrr! Why in the world does anyone not believe me!? I wish Uncle Brutus could of just came out with it! I swear he always leaves me hanging out to dry when I ask him the heavy stuff." As he kicks rocks on the trail while speaking to himself, he noticed one of the rocks he kicked landed on a pile of leaves and branches. He picked up the rock and sees branches were covering up another trail. He moves the branches out of the way and walks down the path. A small hidden area with a square rock facing a cliff captures his attention. "Wow! I found a hidden spot. What a view." Corin takes a seat on the rock. "This is Amazing! I can see the whole village from here. I can even see trees and more mountains. Hey! I can see Kikai's house and mine." Corin closes his eye and puts his hands on his lap. "I think the doctor was right. Having today off isn't a bad idea." Suddenly, loud noises of people screaming were heard from a far. Corin open his eyes and sees fire in the village. "What's that?" He looks closer at the sight of smoke rising in the Sand Lands Village. "OH MY GOD OH MY GOD THAT'S KIKAI'S HUT!" He gets up and bolts it down the trail. He sprints as hard as hard he can to get back. "OH MY GOD I'm coming Kikai! Once Corin made it closer to the village, he sees groups of people wearing black hoods. Just like the man he spoken with the night before. "This must be what he was talking about." He made his way to Kikai's farm through the tall grass. He stays low and out of sight. The large group takes orders from a leader holding a spear.

"Remember everyone. Find that boy and the stone! He can't hide from us. Let's take this island by storm! Don't let anyone leave. Let's send the message we are not to be fooled with. Don't harm the children but take the adults. Split up!" The hooded people begin spreading out into the village. One by one they begin grabbing the villagers and torturing them. Wrecking their cabins, throwing their food at them, making their children cry. Intimidating them with spears aimed towards their necks.

Corin shivers in his sweat. "No way this is happening. All I wanted to do is help make food today with Kikai. Desperate to get to Kikai, Corin evades the group sneakily around the field and trees. "My goodness. I'm almost there." Something taps him on the shoulder. "What?" Corin turns to see two of the black hooded members holding spears.

"Come with us or we will kill you" said one of them.

"Please I just wanted to make food!" said Corin.

The Hooded man chuckled "All you need to know is I'm going to beat you with my bare hands boy!

Corin squints his face right at him. He puts his hands up to defend himself against the two men. "This is going to hurt." Suddenly the two are struck with rocks each directly towards their heads. They fall right in front of Corin's feet. "Huh?" He taps the both them at their shoulders with his foot. "Thanks Jo! You saved my life once again!" Corin smiles at the two laying unconsciously. As he turns to thank Jo, he sees that it was not him. "What the?" WHACK! A wooden staff hits Corin right in the head and he falls to the ground. He opens his eyes to see another black hooded figure looking down upon him.

"Sorry about this" she said. Corin is once again struck in head as he lays knocked out.

Chapter 3 Corin Meets A Girl

The stranger carries the out cold Corin into Kikai's home. Kikai immediately closes the door. She and the Stranger push the table to the side. A door in the floor is opened and reveals steps. The start to go down the steps. Kikai smells the fire on top of her roof. She looks at a barrel full of water. Once she sees the stranger and Corin are safely inside the underground room, she proceeds to light up blue and control the water in the barrel. The water in the barrel rises up and begins to separate. Streaks of water fly all around the once burnt home. In a few short minutes, the magically summoned water finally takes out the flames. "Thank goodness you found him. I was so worried they would kill him." Kikai grabs a bowl of hot water and towel. She begins to clean up Corin's face and wounds. She turns to the table and sits with a smile facing Corin's hero. Kikai stirs her cup of tea slowly and takes a sip. After she sips the tea, she puts the cup down. "Please, sit with me. Could you please take of the hood?" Kikai patiently waits for a response.

The stranger reaches for the hood. The hand stops and the stranger hesitates. "Why do I have to take the hood off?"

"Why save him? Why not just act as horrible as those outside?" said Kikai. The stranger silently stares into Kikai's eyes. Kikai's eyes begin to brighten blue and send blue lines of light towards the stranger. The hands begin to form fists and start to tighten. Kikai sees the stranger body language start to shake. Her blue lights comfort the strangers emotional state and begins to relax. "There is no trouble here. Your safe. I'd just like to know who you are." The stranger unclenches the fists and pulls the hoodie down. Kikai gasps in awe and amazement. "WOW! This is wonderful! You are a…"

Corin wakes up surprised to see Kikai and someone else. "Kikai! Where am I? And YOU! Why did you knock me out with that stick?" Right before he asked, he had a slow moment of being in a beautiful shock gazing upon a beautiful lady. Light brown eyes, short dark hair, lips that makes his heart pound ever so quickly.

She quickly replies "It was the heat of the moment. I did not mean anything by it other than getting us to safety. My name is Seena."

Corin narrowly looks at Seena and Kikai. "Thank you for saving me Seena, but why in the world are you dressed up as one of those invaders out there? How did we end up here in this basement Miss Kikai? What happened to your home?"

Kikai grabs the birthday present. "Slow down Corin. A lot to process I understand. Let us start with this." She hands him it to him. "Open it."

Corin opens it and is revealed to be a blue stone. "This is beautiful. Thank you, Kikai. But what about right now? How are we going to get out of this situation?"

"Stop panicking. Let me drink my tea" said Kikai. Her fingers tap the side of her cup. "You've got to enjoy the moment even if things are going bad. That's gift number two for you." Kikai reaches for her tea and takes another sip. "This is good tea. Let us go back from the beginning. Seena came out of nowhere and saved me from these invaders. They tried to trap me in my home, but she swiftly, sneakily defeated them effortlessly. She is a hero." Kikai then turns to Seena. "Where are you from? Why come here?"

Seena replied "I'm from an island east of yours called Centa. Those "invaders" out there are from Centa. We used to live here on this island a long time ago until the Great Betrayal occurred."

"Again, with this Great Betrayal! At least, I know others know about it" said Corin. He approaches Seena as he holds a cloth over his head. "When I ran back to the village, I heard some of them speak about finding a boy and a stone. Do you know anything about that?"

She looks right at Corin and Kikai with a smirked lip. She tilts her head "Don't know anything about a boy or a stone. I'm just here looking for my missing brother Bravera."

Kikai gasps "That's awful. Let us hope they are not talking about your brother." She continues to drink her tea.

Seena grabs her wooden staff. She leans on the wall and sighs "I really hope not Kikai."

Corin decides to walk over to Seena. She puts her head down and shrugs her shoulders in a stressfully. He leans against the same wall and faces her. "Hey, you saved our lives. Please let us help you Seena."

She looks right at Corin. "It's kind of you really but this is something I must do alone. He told me that he wanted to investigate Mt Hiya and find proof. He wants to clear our people's names and be back on Hope island just like everyone else."

Corin puts his hand on her shoulder. "It's kind of you to think of our safety however, it's too risky for you to be alone." She gives him an annoyed look. "Listen, I may just be a farmer and a cook, but there's one thing I'm good at and Kikai can vouch. Teamwork."

Seena looks back at Kikai. Kikai puts her teacup down. "He won't let you down. Also, you will need a guide for the island. He's the man to do it." She quickly gives him a quick wink without Seena noticing.

Seena sighs at the thought of teaming up with Corin. "You make a valid point Kikai. Okay, were a team." He smiles at response. She quickly grabs the wooden staff. "Don't make me regret this."

"You heard the lady Corin" said Kikai. Now that we have that settled, next tell us more about your brother. How long has he been gone?"

"A month now. Our mother is worried sick and has asked me to find him."

Kikai puts her cup down. "What will they do to him if they find him before you?"

Seena dreads the thought. "They will most likely kill him." "My brother isn't the most well-liked person in our village specifically with our leaders. People saw him steal a boat and one of the commanding officers deemed that as punishable."

"I bet your brother doesn't act without a good reason. Just like you wouldn't come here without a good reason. Blaming others for their mess" said Kikai.

Corin chimes in. "What will we do next? Were fine but everyone else in the village is not. We have to find her brother and help."

Kikai walks over to Corin. "Give us just a moment Seena." Seena sits patiently in the corner and practices with her wooden staff. She grabs Corin "Remember the talk we had last night? Long before I took care of you, I was an adventurer. Looks like today is the day you finally get to explore. Your wish of seeing the rest of the island has been granted." She points at the stone in his hand. "That is your key and your guide out of here."

"How?" Corin responds "Last night you were furious with me about leaving and now your encouraging me? I am happy and confused. Is that normal?"

She laughs "Don't worry about what I said last night. Put it this way your wish came true. It is about right now and you two are our best chance for the people." She raises her voice and waves Seena to come back to the conversation. "You and Seena must head towards the Natura village north into the forest past the gate. My older sister lives there."

"What about you? Come with us" said Corin

"I can't accompany you. I do not have the energy to join you" said Kikai. "You will be fine, trust me."

Seena responds "I'm not here to go to another village. I'm here to find my brother."

Kikai answers back. "Yes, I know. But you will have a better chance looking through the island alongside the best knowledgeable guide in Corin." Kikai grabs a stunned look Corin by the arm. "Listen, I know this all seems crazy but just go with it" She smiles at Seena and looks right back at Corin. She leans into his ear. "She's kind of cute you know."

He looks back at Seena smiling nervously into her serious demeanor. "Okay, I'll go with it."

"HEY!" Seena yells at the two of them. "We should get going now Corin. Before it gets dark out." The three come back up the stairs they came. Kikai closes the floor door.

"Is it safe for you to be up here? What if they try and catch you?" said Corin.

Kikai looks back at the barrel of water and happily smiles as she looks at her fingers. "It'll be fine. You go and find help." For the sake of his own will being, she re-opens the door to the floor.

"Will be back Kikai. Have faith." Corin gives her one last hug. "This time the stone comes with me." He puts it in his pocket and gives her a thumbs up. Seena and Corin sneakily move quietly through the night towards the gate. Their hearts pound loudly. Both of them find cover behind bushes.

Seena puts her hand on Corin's shoulder while pointing at the gate. "So much for getting out before dark. Two things. One, I lead, you follow. Secondly, is that the gate?"

Corin replies "Yes, that's the one." The two see Centa Soldiers capturing women and children. "Seena, are they really going to hurt my people?"

She sighs "Good news is hurting is better than killing. Bad news is they are going to torture the men. For example, that man over there is getting kicked around."

Corin looks in the direction of where she pointed. "That's Jo." Corin pleads with her. "We must help him."

She then replies. "We don't have time for this. We have to get to the Natura Village Corin and find my brother."

He grabs her by the wrist. "Listen, I know you want to find your brother. I need your help. That man helped me the night before after I was attacked. Please."

She takes a moment and observes the surroundings in how to save Jo. She grabs his wrist and takes him down. "Speak but don't grab my wrist or else." She starts pointing and counting at the number of people there. "There's five of them. Hmmmmmm I got it." Seena grabs her wooden staff from her bag. "Okay, Ima go behind the corner near the wall. Once I wave at you, you throw some of these rocks at them. Make them chase you around the corner and I'll take care of the rest."

"Wow, that's simple? Okay, I'll follow your lead." He starts to crouch and sneakily get in position as instructed. He picks up the rocks and puts them in his pocket. She sneakily moves towards the corner of the wall in a stealth like matter.

Corin admires her from a far. "I really hope this works out. I mean the plan works. Yeah that is what I meant. We are going to save you Jo." Once she has gets into position, she looks back at him. She gives her the signal. "Okay, here it goes. Don't miss" Corin begins to lunge the rocks towards the Centa soldiers. He misses the first few throws until he hits one of them in the back of the head.

"Ouch!" One of them screamed. They look around to see who threw the rocks and spotted him. He runs for the corner as the men chase him.

Jo opens his eyes. "What's this kid doing?" he yells. "RUN CORIN!" Jo grabs one of the five soldiers by the foot and yanks him down. "Where do you think you are going weasel. Take this!" Jo pummels the man and proceeds to hold him down with whatever energy he has left to spare. Corin makes it to the corner of the wall.

Seena quickly yells at Corin "Jump!" Corin jumps as Seena commanded while the four remaining Centa men trip over a rope. She quickly knocks them out one by one with her wooden staff.

One of them speaks as he spits out blood. "Seena, how could you help these foolish people and betray your own people?"

She looks into his eyes as Corin aids her by tying them up. "I would do know such thing. I'm here to find my brother, the one you and everyone else wants to kill." She delivers the knockout blows to all four of them with no hesitation. She swiftly strikes them from the knees, the arms, the stomach, the head, without breaking a sweat.

As Corin finishes tying them up, he asks "How long did it take to be an amazing warrior? You do not look the type.

She turns to Corin "Fighters come in all forms. Remember that. I'll tell you more on the way." Your friend." They run back to Jo as he ties up the other soldier. Suddenly, unfamiliar with Seena as she wears similar clothing like the invaders, he quickly reaches for his dagger in hand.

Jo speaks to Seena "What are you doing with Corin?"

Seena responds "We just saved you! I wear their clothes, but I am not your enemy!" Seena reveals her face towards Jo.

Corin confronts Jo "Relax, she's with us Jo."

Jo relaxes and puts away the dagger. He resumes speaking to Seena more calmly. "My apologies, I'm grateful you saved me. Thank you."

Seena does the same as Jo by calming down. "I'm here looking for my brother Bravera. He is from Centa. Think you might have seen someone wandering around here lately that's from there?"

Jo moves his head sideways. "Afraid not Seena, haven't heard anything like that. I just mainly man the gate." He then looks at Corin. "Did Kikai give you that?"

He nods his head and quickly asks Jo. "Yes. How did you know this was Kikai's? She gave it to me as a birthday gift and told me it was important. Don't understand how it's going to help in this intense situation were all in."

Jo looks at Corin and puts his hands on his shoulders. "I've seen a special stone like that before. Definitely isn't one that you just find and hand to someone. No. It's part of something much greater than me and you. I take it she told you to go looking for her sister?" Corin nods his head. "Yeah, just what I thought. Well, I would say wait until tomorrow before you go but due to all of this madness around here, I think it's best you and Seena go now."

Corin asks Jo "What about you and Kikai?"

Jo kicks the man he pummeled. "Don't worry about us. Just get going. My men and I got this now. Ima make them talk and tie them up." Jo walks over to the gate and opens it up. "You two get going and get help! Hope none of the other villages hasn't been invaded yet." He walks over to a cabin and hands them two torches to help guide them through the night. Seena and Corin begin walk pass the gate. Jo closes it up. "Good luck you two. They're going to need it."

Seena has a confused look her face. "I thought Kikai said you were the guide of the island?"

He quickly looks at her. "I am! Just been so long and all. Might be a little rusty."

Seena looks right through Corin as she smacks her lips unconvinced. "Right. Well then, you lead the way. My guide."

Corin confidently walks in front of Seena. "Forward March to NATURA VILLAGE!" They walk side by side into the forest as the night's stars brighten and wolves howling into the nightly atmosphere. The darkness along the gate suddenly rips open for the two.

Chp 4 Kip, Mighty, and Assandra

On the outside skirts of the Natura village, lies a small lookout cabin and a tower. Three individuals are found here with the proud duty of looking for outsiders trying to enter the village.

"YYYYOOOOUUUUUU LLOOOOSSSEEE!!!!" Assandie says.

Kip throws a big tantrum. "I SAW YOU PUT THE ROCK IN THAT CUP! HOW DID YOU DO THAT?"

Assandie smiles right at Kip. "All you got to do is stop LLLOOOSSSIIINNGG and pay attention. She quickly puts the three brown cups down and rotates them at a fast pace. "Okay Kip. Try again."

Kip carefully thinks about his decision. He points at the one to the left. He then points to the one on the right. Kip looks right at Assandie and definitively points at the middle cup with exciting conviction. "IT'S THAT ONE!"

Assandie lifts the cup and the rock is nowhere to be found. "HAHAHA making you lose is too fun!" Kip smacks his knee and gets up. He walks around the room large cabin. Suddenly, he starts stretching and doing push-ups. Assandie stops her constant laughing and puts away the cups. She grabs the little rock and throws it at Kip. "Just say it. I know what you are going to say. Go ahead and say it. For the thousandth time."

Kip picks up the rock and throws back at Assandie. She catches the rock and places it back into one of the cups. "It's been too long Assandie. I want fights and thrills!"

Assandie rolls her eyes at Kip. "Here we go again. You said that yesterday and the day before. What else is new." She runs up to Kip with a quick jab. He counters with a light block and goes for a knee. She side-steps the knee and lightly smacks him on the back of his head. "You want fights, yet you can't spare with me?"

He turns around and puts her in an armlock. He reaches for one of the cups and places it on her head. "C'mon, I'm not talking about this foolery." Assandie giggles at Kip. She rolls out of the armlock and gets back to neutral position facing Kip. "I'm talking about being active. What we used to do. It been almost 20 years since Mighty, you, and I have really done something. I miss it."

She points at a pair of boots behind Kip. He tosses them to her. She sits down and puts them on. After she's done tying the boots, she reaches into her pockets for a string and ties her long hair into a bun. Kip grabs two of the three cups and pours water into them. He hands her a cup. She punches him in the shoulder playfully. "Hey, I get you okay. It's not our fault all of these damn villages decided to hate one another and put up dark magic gates to separate each other. Nobody knows what happened to those great warriors that day. All of them were either killed or disappeared. I say end this hate but who am I to say."

Kip and Assandie walk outside. They stare into the blue sky and the morning sun rise. Kip looks at the ground and lightly kicks dirt at her. "I wonder what life has for us today. Were alive so that's a good start." He looks closely to the ground and sees two praying Mantis fighting one another. He crouches down and pats Assandie to watch alongside him. "Do you remember the last time we were in fight or something like it?"

She looks around and sees little twigs. She places them around the two praying Mantis forming a hexagon keeping them from running away. "Did the time we found those drunks outside the tavern count?" She continues to keep her eyes on the Mantis fighting while drinking her cup of water.

He chokes on his cup of water and begins laughing "Oh god, that was delightfully horrible. They all thought you were seducing each of them into a lovely night until you punched one of them in the gut. So much puke afterwards." She gives him a mean stare. He notices and further explains carefully "But it worked. All of them got to their knees and cooperated with us afterwards. All in their cages." Her facial expression slowly changed to a happier one once he finished his explanation.

Assandie gets up "I'm going to check on the big guy. Enjoy the fight." She walks back into the cabin and sees he is not in his room. She walks around the area and finds him staring off into the distance. He sits underneath a large tree with his left hand out. A red bird lands on top of his arm and comfortably sits there. Assandie decides to sneak up on Mighty from behind the tree. She appears on his right and goes for a kick. The bird flies away as she appears. Mighty catches her foot with one hand just as it was inches close to face and flicks her foot upwards. She falls on her back. He turns to her smiling and happily waves at her. "One of these days I'm going to get you." He walks over to her and sees a small sunflower next to her. He grabs it and puts it in her hair while helping her up. "You are quite the gentlemen Mighty. Why can't all men be like you?" Mighty shrugs his shoulders and starts walking back into the cabin. "Mighty, at some point you will talk again yes? He stops and looks over his shoulder at Assandie. For a split second he appears willing to speak. But decides to resume walking back into his room. She comes back to Kip watching the two praying Mantis fight and sits alongside him. "Mighty still continues to remain quiet. At some point he's going to talk again."

Kip continues to build off the twigs she placed earlier and creates a circle of them standing up. "Mighty is a good guy. Maybe he' going through something. Give him time."

Assandie rolls her eyes and looks at him hysterically "I agree with you, but he hasn't spoken since the Great Betrayal It's been YEARS Kip! Most I have heard from him is laughing. At some point he has got to say something!"

Kip smirks right at Assandie and takes a playfully gesture at her. "Maybe you just LLLOOOSSSEEE in conversation with people."

"Maybe your right" said Assandie. She grabs his cup of water and pours it over his head. "Refreshing talks are the best, aren't they?" She smiles and pats him on the back.

He runs his fingers through his hair "They have their moments. Could you hand me a cloth?" She hands him a cloth and clears his eyes. Once his hair and face have dried up, he sees the sight of two people walking out of the forest towards Natura village. He points at the two. "Do you see what I see?"

Assandie sees the two walking. "I'll get Mighty. How on earth did they get past the dark magic?"

Kip replies "Not sure but one of them has a staff. It's a girl and she's wearing all black. Wonder what that short guy is doing? He is holding a rock in the air. OUCH! He's blinding me with the reflection from the sun! We better act fast."

"This might be the action you've been waiting for" said Assandie. She runs back to get Mighty. Mighty comes out with their equipment in a bag. "I told him they got past the dark magic and he grabbed all our stuff quickly. Terrible talker but great listener."

"Looks like you've been eager for this too Mighy" said Kip. Mighty shakes his head. He puts on his silver gauntlets and an armor plating. He throws Assandie her blade. She puts her blade in her side holster. Kip reaches for bow and arrow. "Aww feels good to have these back on." Kip runs his fingers on a small rope with rocks connected on each end. "Please let them run. I've been dying to throw these again."

Mighty gives a thumbs up to Assandie and Kip. "Okay Kip. We are all ready to go" said Assandie. The three of them move swiftly ahead of the two walking to start planning for the next move. "Okay, how do we approach this. Softly or harshly?" said Assandie.

Mighty and Kip look at each other in a mind reading contest. Kip brushes his hands softly towards Mighty. Mighty disapproves and uses his hands to grip together tightly. After a minute of staring, the two slap hands in agreement. "Harshly is the choice" said Kip. "Alright. Wait until they get closer to the village. Team KMA will please the queen unlike those guards of hers." The three of them begin to set up the harsh moment of surprise for the two.

Corin waves and throws up his stone. He catches it as they continue to walk. "You've been awfully quiet this morning Seena. Something on your mind beside your brother?" She remains quiet. He continues to talk. "I know you can hear me. What is going on in that head of yours?

She abruptly stops. Corin turns around and sees that she is a few steps behind. "Tell me the truth. You lied about being a guide. I don't like lies Corin."

He stops tossing his stone in the air. He walks back to her "I'm sorry. I should have told you from the start. I am about as curious as you are right now about where we are going. This is all new to me. That's the truth."

She further explains. "Trust is important to me. We need to be on the same page if we are to make it through this. Do you understand?"

"Yes, I do" said Corin. They resume walking. He looks at her and thinks to himself. "Damn it, I'm on her bad side. I've got an idea." He breathes a sigh and gets in front of her. "I got into a fight the other day. I was walking home after a hard day's work on the fields as usual I got yelled at and mocked by my fellow villagers about the food. They always make fun of the way Kikai and I cook food for everyone."

Seena puts her hands on her hip and looks at Corin "What does this have to do with right now?"

"Look. You said it yourself. Trust is important. I figure telling you something truthful is a great way to earn your trust back. Let me finish" said Corin. Seena oddly enough lets him speak. "So, the other day was my birthday and I sort of had enough of their constant yapping."

She decides to show interest in his story. "So, then what happened?"

He put his hands in his pockets and kicks the dirt. "I got my ass kicked. It could have gotten way worst if Jo didn't show up."

She begins to laugh. "Now this I believe. I saw the way pleaded with those men before I knocked them out cold." She walks to his side and puts her hand on his shoulder. "Well that's one thing I like about you already, you told the truth. Now I see now why you wanted to help your friend Jo." She raises one of her pant legs up to show Corin a wound. "See that?"

"How did you get that?" said Corin.

"I lied to a food merchant saying I stole the food when it was my brother who did the crime. Don't worry, we got the food to keep us going. We were like ten." Seena winks right at Corin "The girls on the island don't hit hard like me so I was able to take it just fine."

"Let me get this straight. If trust is important, why did you lie for your brother?" said Corin. "Looks like you can't take your own advice." She pulls out her staff in anger. Corin is surprised as she points it towards his head. He mutters knowing she can hit me with ease. He gently puts his hand on the staff and pushes it the side slowly to see her face. "I know you saved me and all, but if I have to learn trust is important as you say, then you should be willing to learn the same as me. No one is perfect, right?"

She takes a moment to gather what he said. She lowers her staff. "I'm sorry." The two continue walking along the trail towards the village. Suddenly, a loud crying noise is heard close by. "Did you hear that? Sounds like a bear cub. It's in pain" Seena looks at Corin as she pulls out her staff. "We should check it out." The two of them head into the direction of the sound. They walk very slowly and crouched unaware of what else is in the tall grass. Buzzing flies begin to freak out Corin.

"Ahh! Bugs everywhere!" said Corin. He pats himself down making sure there is none left on his clothes.

"Lower your voice, were getting closer" said Seena. uses her staff to move the tall leaves out of the way. The two see what that their thoughts are corrects "Wow, it is a small cub. I wonder how it ended up here?"

Corin notices the cubs left foot. "His foot is caught in that ditch."

Seena replies "Okay you help the cub and I'll keep my eyes open. Don't know what else could be out her watching us."

Corin quickly approaches the cub. He kindly pets his head and fur. "Hey there, don't worry Ima get you out." The cub screams as Corin begins to pull the foot out of the ditch. "Easy little baby, I'm almost done." He stops pulling on his foot for a moment and notices it is caught in some roots in the ditch. "Do you have anything sharp?"

She quickly replies "No, I don't. What about that stone Kikai gave you?"

Corin reaches for his stone in the pocket. He begins grinding it against the roots. SNAP! The roots suddenly broke apart and the cub's foot is freed. "It worked!" Corin jumps in joy. He then turns towards the cub. It approaches him and begins sniffing the him.

"Looks like you just made a new friend there Corin" said Seena.

The cub tackles Corin and starts licking him in the face. "Looks like you made quite the impression arrgghh!" Seena quickly falls by the cub and starts licking her face.

"Looks like he likes you too" said Corin. She gets up and holds the cub in her arms. Corin pets the cub. "Sorry If I came off a bit mean earlier."

"It's okay, I should be a lot more forgiving and trusting" said Seena. She puts the cub back to the ground. Corin turns and sees the village. Corin suddenly feels a strange poke on shoulder.

"Seena, please don't hit me with your staff again" said Corin.

"What are you talking about? My staff is in my pouch" said Seena.

"DON'T MOVE!" said Kip. "Tell us why you're here? Your trespassing." Corin puts his hands up as Kip searches him thoroughly.

Seena tries to attack the man but is stopped immediately as she is grabbed by Assandie. "Slow down darling, let the boys do the talking and we have some girl time. Okay?" Kip discovers the stone inside his pouch. "Wow, this is beautiful." He looks back at Corin. "Don't mind if I do."

Corin yells "Hey! Give that back!"

The cub starts to growl at Kip and proceeds to aggressively bites his leg. "OUUCCCHHH!!" He drops the stone and Corin quickly pounces on it.

Assandie for a slight moment is distracted. Seena quickly bites her arm and elbows her in the gut creating a chance to run. "Run Corin!"

The two of them sprint as fast as they could back to the main trail. He looks over his shoulders. "I think we lost them."

Seena and Corin begin to slow down to a complete stop. She pulls out here staff. "We have to be close to the village. They had uniforms and wanted to capture us. We've got to find Kikai's sister."

"Agreed" said Corin. "We are looking for help not trouble. Your brother might be here as well." Loud footsteps approached the two of them as they bunch together.

"Won't catch us off guard this time." Seena gets into her fighter's stance with her staff. Once the figure finally revealed itself, she is in complete shock. "Wow! I've never seen anyone so large before. The bigger they are, the harder they fall!" she rushes in and swings as hard as she possible could but there was no effect. SNAP! The beast raised its left arm up in defense as the staff broke in half upon his arm.

"Way to go Mighty!" Assandie yells as she and Kip make it Mighty.

"Enough of this!" said Kip. He and Assandie pull out long tubes to shoot the two of them with purple pointed tipped needles. In a matter of seconds, both fell to the ground.

 Assandie catches her breathe. She smacks kip in the back of head. "Why didn't we just do that in the first place?"

"It would have been too easy. I love a good chase" said Kip. Mighty picks up the unconscious Seena and Corin. He puts them on a wooden wagon as the three of them happily walk to towards the Natura forest. "Time to be rewarded by the queen."

"Let's stop by the tavern first" said Assandie. "I could use a drink." Mighty nods to Assandie's suggestion.

Chp.5 Queen of Natura Forest

A tall grey castle is seen near the Natura village. It has green vines covering parts of the castle. Inside the castle, two loyal servants of the queen begin to chat.

"Have you seen the queen?" said Kim.

"I swear she was in her room sleeping" said Lilly. Lilly and Kim began to search for the queen. Kim starts walking the first floor of the castle. Lilly takes the stairs and checks the guest rooms. "She's not in here" said Lilly. She walks back downstairs only to see Kim staring into the window. "Hey, did you hear me?"

"I did, just look" said Kim. She points at the flower garden. "Somethings wrong, this is the third time I've seen the queen in the garden. Alone and quiet. Do you think somethings wrong?"

"Would you like to ask?" said Lilly. Kim walks through the kitchen and grabs a plate of bread. She enters the entrance of the garden. Slowly and carefully, she walks over to the queen. The queen is staring at the crosses and tombstones.

"Morning my queen, are you hungry?" said Kim.

She remains focused on the biggest tombstone. "I miss him. I miss all of them" said Nikai. She wipes the tears off her face. Kim offers the bread. Nikai refuses the bread politely. "No thank you Kim."

"The day isn't over." said Kim.

Nikai's eye begin to glow green. She speaks defensively "What did you say Kim?"

Kim takes notice of Nikai's sudden reaction. "He always said that to you. He was there for you and will always be with you even now my queen." She walks closer to Nikai to comfort her. "With respect, you shouldn't be doing this to yourself. The king's death is not your fault. He died protecting the one he loves most." Her words soothed the angry emotions of Nikai to a calmer state of listening. The green brightness of her eyes fade. "Please my queen, find it in your heart to hear my reason of care." She looks over to Lilly then looks back at Nikai. "We are here for you."

Nikai grabs a few of the flowers. A mix of yellow, red, blue, orange, and pink. She lays the flowers in front of the biggest tombstone. "I'm trying my best love."

A guard comes running from the road towards the queen's garden. "My queen! Something awful has happened. There is a large brawl near the village" said the man.

"Gather the rest of the guards in the castle and head back. I'll be there momentarily." said Nikai. The guard immediately runs inside the castle to communicate with the men. "Kim, thank you for your kind words. I'm fortunate to have you and Lilly. I do have one request of you two."

"Anything" said Kim.

"From now on, I'd prefer you call me Nikai instead of my queen." She looks back her husband's tombstone. "He always called me Nikai. I'd fill more of his spirit if you were to do that for me."

"As you wish" said Kim. As the two start to walk back into the castle, ferocious growls occur inside the garden. "Oh my god! What was that?"

 The growls begin to get louder and the creature starts to run towards them. Kim quickly jumps behind Nikai. "Pupooh! Come back here!" said Nikai. She joyfully catches the cub tries running and jumping to her. He tackles her playfully to the ground and licks her face. The scar on his leg did not go unnoticed. "My goodness. You were out in the tall grass again." She puts Pupooh back to the ground and the two make their way to the tree next to the garden. Her eyes began to glow green again and she pointed towards a tree branch. The branch falls off and flies towards her. She catches and lays it to the ground near Pupooh's foot. The green leaves float off the branch and land softly on the scar. The ground started to slowly shake as Nikai pulls out small roots coming out. She took them and wrapped his foot tightly. As she holds his foot, her hands glow green. "Mother's touch against the rough." The leaves and roots fall off the foot revealing the scar is gone. Pupooh happily jumps up to his feet. The winds blow heavily in the direction of Nikai's face. "That's strange. Why does this sound feel so familiar?" She's lost in thought while looking at Pupooh stares at her curiously. He comes to her feet as she pets his head. She gasps at noticing a blue light in the sky reflecting from Pupooh's eyes. "That's the direction of the brawl the guard spoke of. Could she? Maybe. I got a feeling there is something there. Something or someone I haven't seen in a while." She stares at the blue light in the sky wondering to herself "Kikai?"

A large group of men sit happily with drinks inside the village's tavern. "Pour me some more WINE!" said Tobias. The young lady pours the headguard more wine. She feels a slap on her butt as the drunk King. Toby is immediately slapped but laughs as she walks away. He looks back to his men. "I want to drink and toast. To all of the men for remaining loyal to the king."

All the of the King's men raise their glasses to the king. "The KING" They scream.

One of the guards speaks to Toby. "Commander Tobias, what about our queen? The rest of the men look back at Tobias. Tobias looks at all the men and takes a long drink. Slams his cup to on top of the table and laughs.

"Oh! The queen you say. What about her?" said Tobias.

"Shouldn't we be giving a toast for her as well?" said Hans.

Tobias slowly gets up out of his seat. He approaches the guard. "Sorry, but her kind got some of my men killed. Your fellow brotherans." The rest of the men begin to chatter and acknowledge the truth Tobias speaks. "That witch should be lucky to have married the king. Otherwise she'd be dead." The rest of the men roar and cheer for Tobias's strong conviction. The guard at other end of the table sits in silence and confusion.

"We finally made it!" Kip smiles at the look of tavern. "We most certainly need a drink after catching you two. Assandie come with me. Mighty you stay here and watch these two." Kip and Assandie walked inside the tavern for drinks. "Two please. Put it on my tab."

The bartender scoffs "Your overdue Kip! I have let you drink freely too many times. Pay me now or I'm throwing you out!" He grabs a cloth and begins cleaning cups.

Assandie looks at Kip and grins. She turns back to the bartender. "Now. Today is the day. We have something right outside that door that will take of care what he owes you. All we want is celebratory drinks for our big catch!"

The bartender is unphased by Assandie's notions. She puts her hand on top of the bartender's hand in seductive manner. "Relax handsome, we mean what we say." She winks right at him as he begins to blush. "Alright."

He turns around and pours glasses for Kip and Assandie. "My lady, here's your beverage."

"Here you are Kip" said Assandie. She smiles at the two of them and drinks happily.

Kip receives his beverage and raises his glass. He spits it out in shock. "What!? This isn't wine! it's water."

The bartender grins "One drink for her and you'll get yours when you pay."

"Okay I understand. Tell me. Have you seen the Queen?" said Kip

"No, but I'm sure Commander Tobias and his men right over there would now. Looks like they're about to take that fella's head off." Kip and Assandie both move towards the action as they overhear the conversation.

Hans shouts "I don't care what you think of her kind, she's still our queen."

Tobias reaches over for his drink. "As far as I am concerned, I'm king of the Natura Village. I give two shits about that witch in the castle."

Kip begins to whisper. "A witch? Is he calling the queen a witch?" The young lady once again walks over to the table and brings more drink. Tobias carelessly pats her on the butt once more. Assandie snarls after seeing Tobias harass the young lady.

"I'm going to teach him manners" said Assandie. She reaches for her dagger and begins to walk over to the table. Kip quickly gets in front of her.

"Wait. I have an idea. Follow my lead" said Kip. He walks in front of her heading towards the table and raises his hands in the air towards the arguing men. "Hey evening gentlemen. Listen, we hate to interrupt but we need just a minute of your time."

"Do I know you?" said Tobias. He looks closely at Kip and smiles. "I do know you. Your one of the old fighters years ago. Old man we don't have time to listen to a has been so get lost!"

Assandie quickly steps on the man's foot, elbows him in the gut, and grabs his sword. Assandie points the sword near the man's crotch. "If you would like to keep your balls, I suggest you him speak."

Tobias drops his cup. Assandie puts the tip of blade right on his neck. Tobias shivers with his hands out "You have our attention."

He resumes his explanation "As I was saying, oh yes. I'd like to know where the queen is at this moment. We must see her at once. It's very urgent. You're her guards so we take it you would know."

"Tell us the reason first, then will take you to her" said Tobias

Kip walks out of the tavern. "Come Mighty, bring them in" Mighty sighs in disgust and looks at Corin and Seena. He picks them up on his shoulders and enters the tavern. Mighty gently puts Corin and Seena down in front of the guards.

"They are not from around here. What brings you two here in the Natura Village? There's rules on this island" said Tobias.

"I don't care about the rules. Invaders forced me to leave the Sandlands. I'm here to find help my aunt" said Corin.

Tobias looks back at Kip and Assandie. "This looks like a manner my men and I will take from here. Hand them over to us." As the guards get up from the table, they walk towards Corin and Seena. Mighty steps in front of them facing all of the guards in a protective stance.

"Sorry commander Tobias, but we say no." Kip chuckles at the guards. "You see, I maybe old but not stupid. Best we see them to the queen ourselves. Understood?"

One of the men see's Corin's pocket glowing blue. "Look, they have a witch! We must kill them all!"

Tobias's men rush towards Corin and Seena. They are immediately on the ground as Mighty grabs one of them and throws him effortlessly into the rest. Mighty grabs Tobias by the throat. He ferociously throws him into his own Guards. "Get up you fools! Use your swords!" yelled Tobias. The guards swarm at Mighty but Kip and Assandie grabs barrels of wine and throws the barrels at the guards.

"Run!" Yelled Kip. All of them safely made it out of the Tavern. "Whoo that was close. Wait, where's Corin?" The King and his men come out of the tavern with a blade held to the throat of Corin.

"Drop your weapons or I will slit his witch throat." All of them threw their weapons to the ground. Seena narrowly sees past what's behind Tobias from a far. A familiar figure running towards them. Tobias noticed Seena smiling, he turns to see what she could be looking at. He is immediately tackled down and bitten by Pu-pooh.

"ENOUGH! Enough of this violence!" said Nikai. Every man immediately dropped to their knees. Pu-pooh releases his leg and runs back to Nikai. "I demand an explanation" said Nikai.

"My queen! These idiots brought invaders to the village" said Tobias.

Nikai walks over to Kip, Mighty, and Assandie. "Is this true?"

"Yes and no" said Assandie. She steps forward to Nikai. "My queen, they are invaders yes but, we had all of this under control until they decided to attack us for doing our duty in protecting the village.

"We wanted to bring them to you, but commander Tobias refused to cooperate as he has a dislike for you" said Kip.

"Dislike?" said Nikai.

"He said he didn't give two shits for that Bitch in the castle" said Assandie.

Nikai slowly turns her attention to Tobias and the guards. She walks intently towards tobias as the rest of the guards take steps away from Tobias. She looks right into the fear of his eyes. The reflection on his fearful eyes sees bright green coming out of her eyes. His wrists are grabbed by Nikai and roots from the ground rise to tie his hands. More roots and vines appear to grasp the rest of the men's hands. Corin noticed that his stone fell from his pocket in front of his feet.

"Wow, it is glowing" said Corin.

As the others are in awe of Nikai's magic, she turns and sees the blue light right in front of Corin. She walks over to him. Nikai reacts in thought. "How can this be? Only my family of magic can see this glow." She pulls out her very own green stone as it glows along with Corin's. "Please, you and your friends must come to my castle. It is going to be night soon. I need you to explain this."

Corin's jaw dropped. "Yes. Can My friend Seena come too? She needs help finding her brother." Seena's leg is rubbed by Pupooh encouraging her to follow them.

"We could use the rest after all of this" said Seena "What about them?

Nikai turns to Kip, Assandie, and Mighty. "Do you three have a problem with me being a witch as well?

"NO!" said Kip. Mighty nods his head saying no.

She walks back over to the guards and Tobias. "I know I'm hated by half the village because I'm a witch. However, the queen." Her voice raises in tone. "If you refuse to stand by me, then you will face the consequences."

Tobias defiantly spits on the ground and at Nikai. "Your people are the reason why this island is divided. The same reason why my most of my men are dead."

Nikai raises her hands in the air. The roots and vines of the other men suddenly release them freely. She takes one finally look at Tobias. "People are still people. Remember that." The vines suddenly released Tobias for a moment. Nikai grabs one of the roots and forms into a spear. She thrusts the spear directly into his chest. Blood spewed from his mouth. Nikai looks back at the guards "The rest of you are free to go." All the guards ran back to their homes until they were out of sight. Mighty lifts open his shirt and reveals a cut he received from a blade in the tavern "I know of your people. Only a warrior from the mountains can take such pain from a sword." She picks up leaves from the vines and places it on to his wound. "Relax, you'll be fine." The wound disappears. "I will grant the three of you a reward once we arrive at my castle. On one condition."

Kip gradually turns his head towards the deceased Tobias. "Will do whatever it is you ask of us. We are people that value life."

"Good, let's be on our way" said Nikai.

Chapter 6 The family truth

Nikai awakens from her nap in the wagon. "AAAWWWW!" as she stretches her hands out. "We are finally here. Lilly, Kim please make sure to take of care of these three." Nikai then conversates with the others "What are your names?"

Kip speaks cheerfully to the queen. "I'm Kip, this is Assandie, and that is Mighty."

"I'm Corin and this is Seena" said Corin. Everyone stepped off the wagon all at once and headed for the gate entering the castle.

"Lilly and Kim will escort you to your rooms. I will speak to you Corin in private" said Nikai.

Seena whispers in Corin's ear "I will wait for you once you are done."

Assandie notices the two speaking as she comes to Seena's side. "Hey, don't let me be the only girl with these two. C'mon he's in good hands."

Seena smirks right at Assandie of uncertainty. "Yeah, it be nice to get know another girl I suppose."

Lilly and Kim speak to the group. "Come, you are all guests here we have plenty of food and sheets." Everyone followed them to the dining room. All the men began endulging themselves. Mighty, Kip, and Corin rushed to the dining area destroying every dish of food that was on the table. Seena and Assandie slowly reached for food that has yet to be touched.

"Of course, they don't go for the vegetables first." said Assandie.

"Back home this happens all the time. Then we are stuck cleaning up afterwards" said Seena. Both girls begin laughing at one another exchanging different experiences. Mighty noticed the two laughing and grabbed some meat on a sperate plate. He approached them both as he placed food in front of Assandie and Seena. He made eye contact with Seena. The two share a long look at one other. Uncertain of how he would react, she nervously attempts to start a conversation with Mighty. "Hello Mighty?" she said. Mighty looks away and walks out the doors.

"Don't mind him, Seena. He doesn't much talk. We are not sure why." said Assandie.

"Don't worry everyone I'll be right back" said Kip. He gets up out of his chair and follows Mighty.

Nikai comes to the dining room area. "Come Corin. Join me in my quarters." Corin follows Nikai to her study. Lilly and Kim begin cleaning up the area. Seena and Assandie decided to start assist them by grabbing brooms.

"A little teamwork makes dreams work as thcy always say" said Assandie. She looks over to Seena sees her facial expression. "Did I say something wrong?"

Seena smirks right at Assandie "Whoever said were a team?" The two have a face off as the friendly conversating becomes more intense. "If I remember correctly, you three ambushed us and used sleep darts to carry us here. Does that sound like a team to you?"

Assandie quickly raises the eyebrow. She laughs it off and looks right back at her. "Business is never personal. But you make a valid point. I saw the staff you carried. Any chance you'd like to show me your skills?" The two drop their brooms and begin taunting one another.

Lilly interjected "Wait wait wait! No fights in the castle. We are cleaning up."

Seena looks right back at Assandie. "Okay miss business. Tell me. How do we settle this?"

Assandie smiles happily at Seena "We go outside. I saw some wooden sticks out there. I challenge you to sparing of three taps. Should be in your favor since you are familiar with the staff. Or should I say, had a staff."

Seena cringes and huffs at her words about the broken staff. "Alright Assandie. After you."

Assandie replies "Age before beauty." The tension between their eye contact became ferocious towards Lilly and Kim witnessing their back and forth.

Lilly whispers into Kim's ear "My goodness. I hope we get don't get in trouble for this."

 Kim shrugs her shoulders "They are doing it outside. This should be fine. Better there then in here. I am not cleaning up all over again."

 Kip runs on the dirt road to catch up to Mighty. He grabs Mighty by his large arm in worry. "HEY!" Kip yells at Mighty. "Where in the hell are you going? It is dangerous out here in the dark. We need to get back to the castle and await what queen Nikai has for us once she's done talking to that kid." Mighty raises his hand and points towards the fields. Kip notices and tilts his head "Did you leave something in the fields Mighty?" Mighty simply nods his head up and down. "Okay Mighty, go ahead. COME BACK!" Mighty heads further into the direction of the fields, Kip is approached by man with latern light.

"You sir, please follow me." Kip takes a closer look at the man. He approaches him as he leaves one hand on his sword holster.

"Do I know you?" said Kip. Kip stops about 10 feet away from the man. "This is as close as I'm going to get."

The man walks three steps closer and show his face. "You saved me today my friend. My name is Hans"

Kip is stunned by this revelation of who the man is. "Hans, what brings you out here in the middle of the night?"

Hans sighs "I came to speak to the queen. I must inform her of the whispers I've heard." Hans reveals a letter to Kip. "There isn't much time, please listen."

"What is this?" said Kip

"It's a warning. Most of the guards after today feel unsure about being loyal to her. They fear they too will eventually be killed by her." said Hans.

Kip puts away the letter into his pocket. "Does this have something to do with Tobias?"

Hans looks around nervously. He moves closer to Kip and begins to lower his voice. "Yes. Moments before you arrived, the rest of the guards felt the same as Tobias about her. Now that Tobias is gone, I've heard rumors of the guards no longer wanting to serve the queen out of pure hatred."

Kip attentively listens to every word Hans says. He puts his hands together and points his finger at him. "What about you?"

"What do you mean?" said Hans.

'Do you feel the same as them'?" said Kip. "

He takes a moment to think about the question. "I'm not like them. If I were, I would not be out here risking my life to pass this message to her. I'll prove my loyalty to the queen. I'll do whatever is asked."

Kip lightly laughs at his words. Knowing he said the same exact thing earlier in the day. "I believe you. Really, I do. At this very moment, she is speaking to the boy Tobias almost killed. I will personally make sure she gets this." Hans slowly walks backwards. He turns around. "Wait one last thing" said Kip. Kip throws a small knife right in the direction of Hans. Hans freezes in shock seeing the blade fly right in the direction of his face. The blade swiftly passes by his ear. A grunting sound is heard from behind him. Kip starts walking in the direction of where the blade flew. One of the guards from earlier in the day lay on the ground holding his leg. Kip grabs him by the head "Tell your guards to find it in their hearts to stay loyal to the queen and Hans. Do you understand?" The wounded guard nods his head. Kip points at Hans and looks at the guard. "If I find out any harm is to come to him, the rest of you will bleed as your commander did. Got it?" The guard once again nods. Kip's facial expression changes into a cheerful one. "Good. The both of you have a good night. Walk together." Kip pulls out the blade and wipes off the blood with the guard's shirt. Hans and the wounded guard walk back in the direction of the village as Kip walks back to the castle.

"Are you comfortable Corin?" asks Nikai.

"Yes, Queen Nikai."

Nikai rolls her eyes and puffs her breathe. "My young Corin, I hate being called Queen. Just call me Nikai okay?" Nikai pinches his cheeks. Corin takes in the moment observing her as she sits in her favorite chair drinking her tea.

He says in his mind "Wow, she does the same thing Kikai does." said Corin. He then speaks aloud "Do you do that often?"

"Kill you mean?" said Nikai. "No, not often. But I am familiar with it. Only when it's necessary." She decides to change the subject.

"Tell me Corin. Who sent you to me and where did you get that blue stone?" Corin walks over to the window. He sees the view of the Sandlands island from a far.

"Well Nikai, I come from the Sandlands. Just the other day it was my birthday and I was celebrating it with my best friend Kikai. She gave this to me as a gift and said it would aid me in finding her sister. It was too dangerous to stay at the Sandlands. Some strange looking group of people invaded us."

Nikai puts her tea down and smiles. "I'm Kikai's sister which means you found her. That also means you are my all grown up nephew." She stands up and sticks her hand towards Corin. He grabs her hands happily. She then begins to touch his face. "You grew up beautiful like your mother. You have her eyes." Nikai walks over to the window and waves Corin to follow. The two watch from above the sight of Assandie and Seena sparing. "Tell me about your friend."

Corin answers "She came to the island looking for her brother. She dressed as one of the invaders but did it to help me escape. She's an incredible fighter."

"I can tell" said Nikai. "I love the thrill of a good fight."

Corin twist his head at Nikai "How can you hear them fighting if we were in here? I didn't hear a thing."

Nikai answers cheerfully "A little birdie told me."

Corin begins to laugh at Nikai "Hahaha did you say a bird told you?" The two begin laughing together.

"Yes, yes I did. Pretty funny huh?" said Nikai.

Corin finally collects himself. "I think that be amazing except I don't believe you. You had me going there. Birds don't talk."

The two sat right back down. Nikai looks past Corin shoulders as he continues to laugh. A large white, orange, and black-haired owl stands behind him. "Oh, and you humans talk best? I am insulted! Where are the manners? Are they hiding in your pockets?" Lawowl starts hooting loudly.

Corin turns around and jumps back from the owl. "What!? You can talk?" Corin immediately hides behind Nikai. "Who are you? What are you?"

"Yes, I can talk. What I am is the islands protector. My name is Lawowl the Owl. Please to meet you." Corin nervously bows at Lawowl in a friendly gesture. Lawowl turns to Nikai. "My Lady Nikai, did you finally tell the boy what he needs to know yet? It is a pressing manner."

"You came just in time Lawowl" said Nikai. She reaches over for her tea.

Lawowl hops to the edge of the window and watches the fight. "They are so quick. It's rather entertaining."

"Corin, there is more to your life than you know. This is not a coincidence" said Nikai.

He puts his hand on his face. "How come Kikai never told me that I had family outside of the Sandlands? Why now?"

Nikai takes another sip of her tea. She gets up and walks over the wall of her room. She leans on it and faces him. "It was not the right time to tell you yet. We had a falling out years ago. Look, all that matters now is you're here and safe with me."

Corin looks at Nikai and feels a sense of relief. He pulls out his bluestone and rambles on a series of questions. "Can you please tell me what these stones mean? Whatever happened to my parents? Why are there so many stupid rules on this island?" Corin starts to ramble so many questions at a fast rate.

Nikai grabs Corin as tears begin to flow from his eyes. "Listen to me. We were doing it to protect you. Your more than just someone who feeds a village." She starts to tremble as a little tear drips from her face. She struggles to come up with words as it is pain of past emotions arrive through Corin's questions. "Your father was a great man. Braver than any warrior on the island. He trained night and day like I have never seen before. He was also the kindest man I have ever met. He was the only one who could ever make your mother laugh. Then, they had you."

Corin stops crying and looks at Nikai "How did you know I cooked for the village?"

She points at Lawowl sleeping ever so peacefully at the window. "I cannot leave this place to see the island because of the dark magic. As he is my advisor, he believes it is a trap in attempt to kill all who possess magic. Lawowl has seen others in other parts of the island suffering immense pain or death."

Corin continues the questioning. "Why does the Great Betrayal hold such importance to punish everyone now? It's the past not the present."

Nikai walks around the room putting her hands on her hips in the words Corin speaks as he appears much wiser than she anticipated. "You sound like your mother. I mean that in a good way. Instead of finding solutions they resort to blaming and resenting. Specifically, our kind. We are the last of the magical beings here on hope island." She grabs a spare teacup and sets it next to Corin. She pours more tea into Corin's cup. "There is dark magic and foes out there that surrounds the boarders of the villages that's preventing me from leaving. I do not want them to find Kikai. The last of our family must be safe not in danger. I've seen others try years ago to evade the dark magic, but they seem to never return back here."

"Wait!" said Corin. He scratches his head and snaps his fingers. "There was a dark hooded stranger that spoke to me two days ago. He warned me of big changes and vanished. Tell me, did Lawowl see anyone like that?"

Nikai magically grabs a cup of tea and floats it towards Lawowl's nose. He sniffs it and wakes up. "What? No! I did not eat that bread on the table Nikai." Corin chuckles at his response and Nikai answers.

"No. We have not seen anyone like that. But I assure you, I will protect you. Clearly, I'm very capable" said Nikai. She yawns and stretches her arms. "I think it's time we get some rest. We will talk more in the morning. I promise."

"Thanks Aunt Nikai. Sleep is a good idea" said Corin.

She looks over at Lawowl as he is flapping his wings rapidly. "My lady, I think we should go outside! It's getting a little out of hand with the girls." Nikai and Corin rush through the stairs and past the dining room.

"I thought you said we were only going three hits?" said Seena.

Assandie snickers at Seena "What's a matter? You mad I'm going to best you?"

Seena laughs at her comment. "HA! Grandma, you haven't been able to keep up."

 The fight continues to wear them down. The two put their hands out and yell "STICK!" as Leena and Kim both throw wooden sticks for them to spare.

"This is the fourth time they have fought. It's quite remarkable" said Lilly. "At this rate they can make all the wood we need for the winter and have many fires to enjoy. Together." Lilly grabs Kim's hand and smiles at her happily. Kim blushes back at the romantic gesture.

Nikai walks up from behind Kim and Lilly. She notices the two having an intimate exchange. "Enjoying the night so far?"

"Oh God!" said Kim. "Sorry Nikai, we were just.."

"Enjoying the night. It's okay" said Corin. "Happiness should be expressed, not hidden." Nikai shows a small smile at the compliment Corin made for the two.

"Nicely done" said Nikai.

Seena and Assandie's sticks continue to collide many of times until a unsettling noise occurs. "SNAP!" Both sticks broke in half instantly.

 "Well, looks like it's over" said Assandie. She starts to walk towards the castle. Seena swiftly cuts in front of her.

"Were not done yet" said Seena. She lifts her hands up making fists towards her. Assandie holds her hand in pain.

"Listen, you made your point. You win" said Assandie. Seena turns away and waves at the group. As she turns her back, Assandie quickly twist Seena's arms and side-step trips her to the ground. She pulls out her dagger and presses it against her throat. "Never ever underestimate your opponent." Assandie lifts the blade off her throat. She helps Seena up. "Grandma taught you how to fight Seena?"

Seena replies "No, it was my brother." Assandie stops and looks at Seena. "He's a good brother for teaching you."

"I hope he's still alive" said Seena.

Assandie gives her a look "Did you say alive?"

"Yes, I absolutely did I'm here to find him and bring him back home" said Seena. Assandie keeps a mental note of her answer. Finally, the two walked side by side with Assandie's arm on Seena's shoulders. Everyone gave them a round of applause. Nikai made sure she was the first to speak.

"So, who won?" said Nikai. The girls looked at each other.

Seena tries to answer Nikai but is immediately cut off by Assandie. "Seena won. At the end I was critiquing her on new possibilities to look out for."

Nikai was pleased with Assandie's answer. She then turns to Seena. "Is this true?"

Seena replies "Yes, Nikai. She was being a good teacher after all."

Nikai smiles at them cheerfully "Well, you both put on quite the show. But the show must end now. We must all get some rest. Got a big day ahead of us tomorrow."

Corin quickly intervenes "What's going on tomorrow?"

"The only other time I ever saw you was when your mother gave birth to you. I'd like to catch up with my nephew" said Nikai. She quickly turns to Seena. "Don't worry. I will help you find your brother. Family is important."

"Thank you" said Seena.

Chapter 7 The Lost Friends

Nikai tosses and turns in her bed. She gets up and walks over to her green stone that sits on top of her dresser. She picks it up and grasp it tightly. "One day sister, we will be back together."

Lawowl flies into her room as he gracefully lands. "Good Morning My Lady! Ready to get started on the day?"

She puts her green stone down. "Not really. I'm thinking about my conversation with Corin last night."

Lawowl flies to the corner of her dresser. "Could you elaborate further?"

"Two days prior to him arriving to our village, he spoke of a man in dark clothing visiting him" said Nikai. "You were asleep when he mentioned it. Did you see anything of that sort last night?"

Lawowl fluffs his wings "I did see something last night. Two men. A large one and a not so large one wandered off last night. The large one headed towards the Tall Grass fields while the other was talking to a stranger in the middle of the road. Where you aware of any of this Nikai?"

"Yes, I was aware of the two leaving and returning back here. A stranger? Those two along Assandie downstairs expect to be rewarded for their efforts for bringing Corin and Seena to me."

Lawowl gives a squinted stare at Nikai. "I am suspicious of those three Nikai. Something isn't right about them or any of this.

Nikai tilts her head "Why do you feel this way? They have cooperated with me so far. Definitely didn't call me a Bitch neither."

Lawowl interrupts "After you executed commander Tobias, I don't think anyone should attempt to insult you Nikai."

She comes close to Lawowl and begins petting his feathers. "I understand Lawowl. I say keep a close eye on Kip. The smaller one you described. From a distance. He may have been talking to someone who may be looking to steal the stones Corin and I have."

Lawowl flies to the ledge and turns his head towards Nikai. "I will do as you say my Queen." He bows and flies off

Nikai puts her hand on the palm of her forehead "God! You know I don't like being called queen!"

Lawowl flies back to her and gives a playful wink. "I'll be back later and let you know if you find out anything. I will see to it. As Lawowl flies off, she prepares to go about her day with Corin and the group. She calls for Kim and Lilly to prepare her clothes and bathing water. As she enters the bathing water Kim and Leena prepared for her, she tells them to check in on everyone downstairs. Her thoughts begin to wander and eventually she speaks to herself "I hope this means I will be reunited with my family soon. It has been so long. I miss Kikai."

Corin awakens from his sleep and yawns. As he slowly gets up from his bed, he noticed an empty bed. "Seena? I wonder where she went." He begins putting on the rest of his clothes and walks around the castle looking for her. He sees Assandie sitting alone reading a book of poems. "Good morning Assandie. Have you seen Seena?"

Assandie replies "Good morning Corin. I have not seen her. Have you seen Kip and Mighty?" Corin shakes his head and shrugs his shoulders. Corin hears a scream outside. He runs past Assandie and heads towards the noise.

"What's all the screaming about Seena?" said Corin. His eyes lay on the sight of Seena and Mighty in front of one another.

She turns to him "He fixed my staff. How, did he do it?" Seena shows Corin the once broken staff that has blue markings on it. "Looks as if it was never broken but it was!" She begins practicing her movements with it. Mighty grabs a big rock on the side of the dirt road. In an effortless manner, he lifts it up and walks over to Seena. Mighty lightly pats the large rock and taps it. He then proceeds to point at Seena and tap the rock.

"I wonder what he is saying?" Seena said.

Corin replies "I think he wants you to go to the large rock Seena." She walks up to the rock. She then looks back at Mighty. Mighty then begins to form a fist hand gesture holding a weapon and swings his hand. "Looks like he wants you to swing at the rock with your staff Seena."

Seena looks back at Corin "Why would he want me to do that? He just fixed this for me and know he wants me to break it again?"

"Just do it Seena" said Kip. "I've known him for years. Mighty doesn't things without a reason."

Seena looks back at Mighty and sees him hands awaiting her to hit the rock. "Okay, here it goes." She closes her eyes and swings the staff as hard as she can. A loud snap occurs. Her eyes remained closed and her grip on the staff remains firm.

"Open your eyes Seena!" Corin yelled.

She opens her eyes and looks immediately at the staff in her hand. "My staff! It's fine." She turns to see in front of her the once large rock is now cracked into many pieces. She yells "AMAZING!" in pure joy. She runs to Mighty and gives him a hug. "Thank you Mighty".

Mighty looks at Kip. Kip replies "Don't look at me Mighty. Look at her. Say you are welcome. Or something along those lines."

Mighty instead hugs her back with a joyfully. She pinches him on the cheek and laughs.

"Nice to see she has a soft spot" said Corin. As he continues adore the two having a good time, he notices Assandie walking outside and is surprised to see Mighty showing affection. Assandie's smile is soon disappears as Kip grabs her by the wrist and

"We need to talk. In private" said Kip. Kip and Assandie walk further away from the castle and group to speak in private. Corin sneakily follows them from a safe distance to eavesdrop. Kip points his finger at Assandie in excitement. "Assandie, we may have a situation. Do you remember the man we rescued at the Tavern the other day?"

Assandie nods her head "Yes Kip, I remember clear as day why?"

"I spoke to him last night. His name is Hans. He informed me there is whispers that the remainder of the guards are having second thoughts in being loyal to Queen Nikai."

"I can see why. Better yet, we all saw why" said Assandie. She sees the letter Hans gave to Kip. She quickly snatches it from his pocket. "Tell me, what's the catch. I know you. There is always a catch. Nobody doesn't do anything for anyone unless there's something in it for them."

Kip replies "I think it would benefit us if we refused the reward."

Assandie slaps Kip. "What! I want to the reward. This does not sound like you. Do you like staying at the scouts cabin all the way out there? I hate it."

Kip rubs his face softly and looks back at her. "No, I don't like it there which is why I suggest we do this. We ask to be her new set of guards."

Assandie scoffs "Might I remind you that she killed her former commander of the guards in a matter of minutes in front of us. I'm not sure if this is a good idea."

Kip snatches the letter back from Assandie's hand. "With this letter, it'll be fool proof. I saved Hans last night. He nearly got killed by one of those bastards. It's proof enough for me to see we need to make this move." He points over her shoulder. "Look at him. Mighty is happy. Don't you want to be happy to Assandie?"

"What about what you said before about action?" said Assandie. "I see what you mean, but what if we are killed the same out of a disagreement? There's no way we can stop her." Her voice starts lower as she ponders on a thought outloud. "The one time I let my guard down, my daughter paid the price she was murdered by a monster. It should have been me."

Kip shoves her to break the thought absorbing her negatively. "You are not alone in losing family. If she wanted us dead, we would be dead already. See reason in my words. Will find justice for our families.

Assandie quickly throws a right hook and trips Kip with her feet. As he falls to the ground, she pulls out her dagger and leans it against his eye. Her voice erupts in anger loud enough for everyone to hear miles away. "DON'T YOU EVER SPEAK OF THE FAMILIES TO ME AGAIN! MY DAUGHTER IS NOT COMING BACK. WHAT I SAW OF THOSE EVIL THINGS DOING TO OUR PEOPLE WAS SOMETHING THAT STILL HAUNTS ME! FOR ALL YOU KNOW HE MIGHT BE WITH THEM!" Blood begins to leak from Kip's face. Her anger blinds her clear thinking and then questions him. "Are you one of those things, Kip? Cause if you are, I'll finish you off right now."

"Have you gone mad? Stop! Assandie it's me!" yelled Kip. He grabs her wrist and pushes it away from his neck as far as he could. She continues to press back. The tip of the blade touches of his throat.

"Assandie stop! You are going to kill him! said Corin. He rushes to Kip as fast as he could. He pushes Assandie off him. In a crazed state, she rushes towards Corin. She dashes towards him in a blind rage and lunges at him in the air. Seena runs in the nick of time and pokes her out of the air with her staff. She immediately falls to the ground gasping for air

Assandie gets up and continues to be enraged but is soon grasped by Mighty. He holds her with one arm and reaches for her dagger with the other. After a few more attempts to break free of his grip, she finally gives up.

"Let me go of me now Mighty, I need space" said Assandie. Mighty grunts in dissatisfaction of her behavior. She looks at him in a calmly manner than moments before. He slowly lifts his arms off but keeps them up in case she moves violently again. She walks back into the castle and locks the door of her room. Emotions overcome her as she falls to her knees crying aloud. Nikai walks by her room and slowly stops to listen to her weep for her daughter. "My little light. Why didn't they take me instead?"

Corin helps up Kip and hold him upright as he walks over to Mighty. "You need to tell Nikai all of what you know. I heard everything."

"You give this to her" said Kip. He reaches into his pocket and hands him the letter Hans gave him. "I need to walk away this off. I brought up painful memories."

"Are you capable to walk?" Said Corin.

"Yeah, I'll be okay. I'll head back to the fields. Get something that will help ease her mind" said Kip. They make their way to Mighty. Mighty takes a long stare him as Kip knows he said something wrong to upset her. He puts his hand Kip's shoulder and points in the direction of the tall Grass. "You know me so well big guy."

"What are you going to do Kip?" said Seena.

"I'm going to take a long walk back and get her daughter's necklace" said Kip. "She's not one for apologies but this will have to do."

"You sure about this? It'll be dark out by the time you get back" said Corin.

"I could use the exercise. Do me a favor kid. Keep an eye on her for me." said Kip. He begins to walk towards the road. "Better hurry before it gets dark."

Chapter 8 Trouble Ahead

Mighty and Corin walk into the castle dining area. They join the already seated Nikai, Assandie, and Seena speaking amongst themselves. Corin asks Nikai "Aunt Nikai, there is something you need to know…" He hands her the letter Kip gave him. She opens it and quickly glances at it. She puts it in the middle of the table.

"A small piece of writing droves everyone mad I see" said Nikai. "Looks like our day together Corin will be put on hold due to this current eventful morning." She turns to Assandie and gives her a smirk. "Isn't that right Assandie?"

"I apologize Nikai for my behavior." said Assandie

"I'm afraid that's not going to do. Stand up." said Nikai. She gets up from her seat and walks up to Assandie. The two have an intense stare down. The tension in the room is felt as emotions begin to run high. Lilly and Kim put their hands flat on the table. Mighty crosses his arms. The cold winds from outside began to enter the castle and chills were felt all over. She sees Assandie's fingers tapping the handle of her dagger. "You want to avenge your daughter. Do it. Here, let me help." Nikai's eyes light up green. Vines begin to appear from the ground. One of the vines grabs Assandie's sword and places it in her hand. She becomes hesitant and freezes at the opportunity of killing Nikai.

"ENOUGH!" yelled Seena. She quickly strikes the dagger out of Assandie's hand with her staff. Corin walks over to Nikai. She stands right in between her and Assandie.

"Seena is right" said Corin. "Fighting one another will not help. We must work together. Understand."

"I was wrong to act out of anger" said Assandie. "I shouldn't be here." She picks up her dagger and begins to walk away.

Nikai's green light begins to disappear. The vines slowly go back to the ground. "We want the same thing." Assandie stops walking. "I understand your loss. The great betrayal has hurt all people of the island." She walks back towards Assandie. "I cannot apologize for the heinous act my kind did to you. But If you stay, I will do everything in my power to make sure no one is ever going to feel pain like that again. Justice and answers." Assandie takes a good look at Nikai's face. She nods and walks back to her seat. Kip's words rung in her head louder and clearer as it has given realization of what is needed.

"Allow us to be your new guards. Danger seems to follow us now since the messenger was nearly killed trying to pass this information to you" said Assandie. She looks at Mighty. Mighty approves the request by giving her a thumbs up.

"Very Well" said Nikai. The two shake hands. Everyone in the room felt at ease seeing the two putting their differences aside for the greater good. "You need to know the whole truth Corin."

"I'm listening" said Corin.

"It's about your father and mother" said Nikai. "Long before you were born, your father and you mother fell in love. He was a good man who fell in love with a gifted woman. It created controversy on the island as he was a human and she was not. Our family was divided by it."

"What was his name Nikai?" said Corin.

"His name was Corvan. he was the greatest fighter the island has ever seen."

"He was one of the greatest yet" said Assandie. "There were others as well. I've heard stories of him through the men he defeated that were part of my village east from here."

"What happened to him and the others?" said Corin. "Why is everyone not allowed to walk the island freely like before?

Nikai eyes glow green in anger at the thought of having to explaining the hardships. The ground starts to shake due to Nikai's emotions. Memories of the good days came to her mind.

"Let me do it" said Assandie.

"Years ago, at Mt. Hiya, people discovered our greatest warriors dead with no reliable truth as to how. What happened next was ongoing conflict causing separation between us all. The hooded men were defeated but we believe some were missing. Specifically, Corvan. I believe there is more to this."

Seena loudly taps her staff to the ground making a small crack to collect everyone's attention "I don't mean any offense, but I came here looking for my brother"

"How long has your brother been missing from your homeland?" said Assandie.

"Two months ago. I disguised myself as one of the centa soldier in the Sandlands just to get here without anyone noticing""

Assandie draws a face of concern and confusion. She and Mighty look at each other then look back at Seena as if she were mad. "I'm fully aware of the ways of Centa people and they are good people. Why would they come to this island and invade the Sandlands tribe?"

Nikai asks "What did their faces look like?"

"Nikai, they looked soulless" said Seena. "The things I overheard befuddled me. Hurt them. Find the stones. Serve our king. My face was hidden so I could blend in. The hatred sounded unreal to me. Their eyes looked lost as they spoke. As if they were in a trance. My heart was breaking hearing them as my mother and father knew some of them growing up. They would never say such hateful things. But they did"

Corin mind slowly gathers everything being said around him. The memory of that mysterious man immediately came to mind. "Assandie!" She turns to Corin. "Did you say hooded men?" The night before all of this happened, a black hooded man spoke to me."

Assandie's expression was shock that everyone felt in the room. "Impossible! We extinguished them long ago!" She tries to read his face. "How are you still alive? You actually had a conversation with one of them!?"

Nikai steps in "Calm down Assandie! Give Corin a chance to speak." Nikai comes to Corin "Tell me nephew, what did this hooded one say to you?"

"He asked me if I knew who I were" said Corin. He trembles fearfully at the thought of being killed. "I'd like to live a lot longer."

"You will not die because of the family that failed you" said Nikai. "These stones, our kind, will live long and things will go back to the way they once were."

"And what if they don't?" said Assandie.

Nikai hears Pu-pooh calling for her. She runs outside to the yard. "What's wrong Pu-pooh?" Pu-pooh stands on his feet and raises her paws as high as he can. Lawowl is seen in the night's sky flapping his wings looking down at Nikai as he aggressively scans the land.

"NIKAI! Great danger is coming! Great Danger is coming!" he shouts. "A large group of people are heading this way!" The others overheard Lawowl's screaming and rushed outside to see what was going on.

Nikai replies "What did you see? How long do we have before they get here?"

Lawowl flies down to Nikai hover closer to her face. "Twenty minutes at the most. I saw a group of them taking out one of the old guard posts. They have captured Kip."

Assandie stomps the ground in frustration. "Shit. That was our post. So stupid to have lost my temper. This is my fault."

"No, it's nobody's fault" Nikai said. "It's clear to me that they are trying to kill what's left of our family." She turns to Corin. "I'm sorry all of this is happening so fast and there is little time to explain. To everyone." Nikai quickly turns to Lawowl. "Lawowl, I need you to fly fast as possible and alert all of our guards to come her immediately." Without any hesitation, Lawowl quickly nods and flies upward to the sky. "Pu-pooh, I need you to go to your favorite hiding spot okay." She gently pets the cub and kisses her on the forehead. Pu-pooh runs off. Nikai turns around to the others. "Listen to me. Neither I or any of us can do this alone. I beg for your help. To protect the innocent ones in our village."

 Mighty and Assandie step forward. "Were going to make this right" said Assandie. "It's been an uneasy time today. Never thought I'd ever get a chance to fight alongside magical beings. Let alone two."

"As my King once said, there is a first time for everything" said Nikai.

Assandie comes over to Seena. "Looks like are warm up sparring will be put to the test out there."

"My brother may be with them. If they lay harm to him, there will be hell to pay" said Seena.

"That's the proper spirit" said Assandie. She sees Mighty coming up Nikai. "What's he doing?"

Mighty comes to Nikai. He puts his hands out to her. Nikai notices his hands glowing blue. She is in awe at what she sees what Mighty is trying to do. Nikai grabs his hands gently. For a long minute, the two closed their eyes. Nikai hears Mighty's voice between their minds. "I will protect Corin. No matter what. My queen."

"Understood Mighty" said Nikai. They open their eyes and let go of each other's hands.

"What on earth did they just do?" said Seena.

Nikai explains "We spoke to each other through our minds. He will guard Corin is what he said."

Assandie claps her hands. "Hey! Let us get ready to prepare for this everyone." Everyone begins to head back inside the castle. She quickly puts her hand in front of Mighty's walking direction. "Mighty, I'm happy to see you looking like your old-self again old friend." Mighty's smile quickly turns into a confident look. He forms a fist with one hand and puts the other hand on Assandie's face. He grunts with a look of support towards Assandie. She puts her hand on his fist. "Were going to get Kip back.".

Chapter 9: The Hooded Men:

In a land that is high in the mountains of Hiya, two hooded men speak as they look upon the lands of the island. "Hope Island. What a funny name for a place that is the opposite now." Mustar walks along the edges picking up rocks and throwing in the direction of the trees. "Cannot wait to have it all Kustar. Do the deeds for our king of the mountains and we will have complete control."

"Then what? What happens after that?" said Kustar.

Mustar grunts and sighs. "Here we go again. Listen, when the king controls the island, he will give us what we deserve. Our loved ones. Don't you want to see your family again?"

Kustar angrily reacts to Mustar. "I hope your right about this Mustar. Hope this King of ours can keep his word. This island has a history of people not keeping their word. The Great Betrayal says it all."

Mustar begins to laugh "Ha-ha ah yes, the truth in that is right but hey it wasn't our problem to begin with. Just be glad we weren't on the other end of those blades."

"That's one way of looking at it" said Kustar

A group of red clothed servants signifying their rank below Mustar and Kustar approached them. "Mustar and Kustar. The King asks for your appearance at once" said the red servant.

The two men walk to the Dark temple covered in green roots. As they entered the Kings palace, noises all around are heard pleading for freedom.

"Look at them Kustar! Our pets think they deserve freedom." Mustar comes up on the cages and kicks it laughing psychotically. "Will let you out when we feel like it!" Eventually they make it to the steps near the king's throne.

The royal guards of the King approaches Mustar and Kustar. "Kneel" they say to Mustar and Kustar. The king stands tall in his black and gold attire. He opens his hands and arms towards them.

"My servants, Mustar and Kustar, have you found the stones yet?" said King Feroick

"No King Fearrick. No sign of them yet" said Mustar.

The King walks past them with a smirk. He politely asks one of his servants to bring him a beverage. "Those stones are out there you two. Once we have them, our arrangement will be complete, and I shall bring your loved ones back to life. Time is short for us. We must find them soon."

Kustar sharply asks "Tell me something King Fearrick, what if weren't able to find these stones, then what? Is there another plan? Because if there isn't"

Fearrick quickly turns around and throws his beverage in the air. The beverage in mid-air slowly comes out. He puts his hand out as black energy comes from his body towards the liquids into a sphere pointing right at Kustar's Neck. "The other plan is death. For both of you." A servant approaches King Fearrick. Presents him another drink. He graciously receives the new drink, the sphere formed from dark magic disappears. The king walks back to his throne. "Forgive me, I'm growing impatient and frustrated of the search."

Mustar calmly asks the king "Is there more on the line than your letting us know? About the purpose of finding these stones?"

Fearrick turns to Mustar and says "Yes, there is more of a purpose. Twenty years ago, at the end of the Great Betrayal, I discovered that my son has gone missing and my wife is in deep unbreakable comma. Only with the power of the blue stone I be able to find my son and awaken my wife. Be whole with my family again." He looks at Kustar. "I wish I could be out there looking, but I cannot leave this place. The Gods have forbidden me to leave. If I disobey them, I will lose the powers I have earned through their trust. Which is why I'm in need of your services."

Kustar tilts his head. "King Fearrick. So, you care more about being a King than being a father?"

As the two hold a stare down of intense tension, one of the guards runs up to the three having their stalemate of a confrontation. "King Fearrick! Mustar and Kustar! Some prisoners escaped!

King Fearrick yells "Find them at once!" Mustar nods and runs with the guard to chase after the prisoners. Fearrick yells once more "KUSTAR". Kustar stops and turns around. Fearrick raises his hand as dark energy beam hits his forehead. "I will no longer be taking these questions or remarks from you no more! Choose wisely. Serve? Or Death?"

Kustar falls to his knees as he is overpowered by Feroick's dark power grasping him by the throat. His eyes turn black as they were once brown. "I will serve you and only you King Fearrick."

"Good Kustar. Now, off you go!" says Fearrick

In the clear distance further away from the King's Temple, two prisoners are running for their lives towards the exists. "How in the world did we end up here?" said the bearded prisoner. "One minute I'm at home with my wife and children, the next minute I pass out and end up here in this place full of torture and screaming." "What about you? Remember anything before all of this?"

The younger man of the two men with black long hair and Centa village clothing replied "I remember hugging my sister Seena and telling her I must return to this island for answers. Once I arrived on this island, I traveled deep into the island from the Sandlands to the mountains. Next thing I know, Two, black hooded men surprised attack me and I woke up in a cage."

The bearded man turns around and sees behind him others chasing the two. "Like those two behind us?"

The young man turned around and said "Yes! It was those two exactly!"

The three of them made it all the way to the exit until the rest of the guards appeared at the other end. All the guards along with Mustar and Kustar surrounded them in a circle preventing them from any chance of escaping. One by one the guards ran towards them with bare fists and swords. The young man out of the two showed no fear as he prepared to set his feet in a fighting stance while the other showed no knowledge or experience in fighting. "this time you will face me not cowardly strike me from behind" said the young man. In a matter of seconds, he took on the incoming guards and swiftly dodged their attacks and countered them flawlessly with kicks, punches, and grabs throwing them into each other. As he hooked one of the guards to the ground with his fist, a sword fell to the ground and he picked it up. He throws it to the one who doubted the situation and yells "Hey! Stand and fight with this!" The two men fought for their lives, Mustar and Kustar watches on.

"Impressive skills. Haven't seen anyone fight like that before" said Kustar.

Mustar turns in annoyance to Kustar. "Are you admiring him or are we going to put an end to this?"

Both men suddenly stopped talking as they see all the guards laid down to the ground.

"Where did they go?" said Mustar. He walks up to one of the guards still on the ground. "Defeat was not supposed to happen!" He grabs their sword and stabs the wounded guard in the chest. In frustration, he pulls out the sword and points at the remaining guards. "The next time any of you fail me, I'm killing all of you." Mustar notices the dark look in his eyes Kustar possesses as he yells. Shocked at the sight of his friend's look, he also noticed a trail of blood leading towards the entrance. He followed it seeing that it ends near the cliff. As he looks closer at the cliff, he sees the two men climbing towards a top of a hill leading towards the forest.

Kustar appears next to Mustar. "Were not done yet." King Fearrick's voice took over Kustar's voice and spoke to Mustar. "Your friend needed some adjusting to my demands. You don't need to worry unless you want to follow the same path as he did." Mustar gulped in shock and nodded no. "Good Mustar. Now that we have gotten that out of the way, both of you will follow them down and kill them. I received word from one of my scouts they could be heading towards the Natura Village. Go now or I will kill Kustar."

Kustar suddenly realizes he's facing Mustar with a blade on his neck. He puts the blade down and ask Mustar "What happened?"

Mustar answers "King Fearrick wants us to go after them. They are heading into the Natura Forest. C'mon let us go before nightfall."

Chapter 10: What Lies Ahead

Meanwhile back at the Sandlands….

Jo walks around the village while yelling at his men. "Come on men. Check every home. Make sure there is no intruders hiding. We can't have any more of these crazy invaders ruining our village!" He comes by Kikai's place and sees the outside of it. "Oh my god. It is a damn shame. I hope that Corin kid is alright." As he looks in awe and concern of the fire damage done to the place, he suddenly hears a noise inside. "Oh no. Not going to let them get away! Men! Come here I need a few of you to help take some these invaders." Jo's men came with spheres and swords ready to step inside Kikai's place. Jo opens the door forcefully and the rush right in.

"My Goodness! Don't hurt me!" said Kikai "I was just trying to make some breakfast." The men calmly walked outside as Jo stayed inside with her.

"Are you alright? Are you hurt?" said Jo. "These people really did damage to our village. Breaking personal items and hurting loved ones." Jo joins Kikai at her table as she prepares some tea and bread. She offers him tea and bread. "Sorry to have startled you. May I join you? I haven't eaten lately."

"I insist. Company would be nice" said Kikai. She points her finger at him "You need to keep your strength up. I know your duty is to protect but you need food to stay strong."

Jo is destroying the food joyfully like there is no tomorrow. He happily looks back at her with food all over his beard and face. "Beautiful and caring."

Kikai snickers. "Tell me, how bad was it out there? Is Corin and Seena alright?"

Jo stops chewing and swallows the food. He chugs up all the tea in the cup offered to him. As he wipes his face of joy, he says "Real bad. Thankfully, no one was killed. A bunch of wounded. Corin and Seena saved my ass out there. The girl really knew how to handle herself. They are okay Kikai. Corin and Seena went to the Natura Village looking for someone you told him to find."

"Good, I'm glad they are fine and far away from here" said Kikai. She walks up to the door and checks out the village. She sees a boy running to her place as fast as he can. He immediately stops in front of her as he catches his breathe.

"Excuse me miss, I need to see my dad Jo." Said Mikken.

Jo gets up and walks up to the door. "Son, you looked like you ran all over the island. What is going on?"

"Those invaders. You have to see this seriously." Jo and Kikai walk past Mikken. The three of them walk the dirt trail heading up to the gate. "Dad, this is weird. One minute they're saying "We must serve our master and find the stones. Now they're saying let me go!""

Jo and Kikai wonder why the sudden change of behavior. "Kikai, Corin mentioned you gave him a stone. I wonder if they're after that blue stone" said Jo. Jo runs towards the gate where the tied-up invaders where the backs are on the gate. He approaches one of them constantly babbling. "Okay, why is my son telling me you want to leave? Do you not realize you all pummeled me two nights ago? I need answers?"

The man spoke up. "Sir! We have no idea how we got here. We were at home in Centa just living our normal lives and everything goes dark. We didn't mean to harm anyone!"

Jo looks back at Kikai as she seems concerned. "Kikai, do you have anything you can tell me that can make sense of this."

Kikai looks right at Jo with her heart racing. Her hands begin to sweat as she screams in her head. "They were dead. How in the world can they still be alive?" She shakes her head out of the deep thought in her mind and looks back at Jo. "This is the work of the hooded men. The dark magic that plagued the island during the Great Betrayal. Never thought this would be happening once again."

Jo takes a moment to let it sink in. He turns around and looks at all them men tied up with worried faces that long for freedom after being controlled by a dreadful experience. "This is not how I'd imagined all of this going down. Mikke, grab my knife. Can't take any chances." Kikai and Mikke gasps. He grabs his father's knife and hands it to him. Jo points the knife right at one of them "Aware or not Aware, you Centa people must pay for the harm caused here." Jo swiftly slashes the ropes one by one of all the men tied up. "Mikken, go with the rest of my men. Find them and tell them to free the rest of them." Mikken nods and runs off doing his father's request. He then turns back to Kikai. "Look, I'm not a know everything kind of man but I know your different. I've always known."

Kikai shrugs her shoulders and sighs looking up. "Yes, I'm afraid so. I am a magical being. Well one of the last ones remaining. How did you figure it out?"

"Let's just say I have experience with special individuals" said Jo. "you sent Corin off with a bluestone towards the Natura Village. I've magic like things when I see it. Jo walks up to her as he sees her expression of guilt. He slowly comes up to her. "Hey, I'm not judging you. I accept you as Kikai the magical lady who makes us food."

Kikai begins to laugh. "Tell me, does the magic make the food taste that good? Cause if it does, I'm not fussing."

Jo noticed how her mood changed to a more relaxed state. "Corin is a good kid. I can tell by his manners and the way he speaks you had something to with that. That means something you know."

"He is a good boy indeed" says Kikai. "It's been tough raising him and teaching him. He is like the son I have always wanted but the truth is I am his Aunt. We kept a promise to his mother and father that we would look after him before the Great Betrayal happened."

"We?" said Jo. "I see you, who's the other?"

"My sister Nikai in the Natura Village. She's a queen there."

"Why didn't you just come with Corin and Seena to the Natura Village? Wouldn't you want to see your family again?" said Jo.

She crosses her arms and sheds a tear. "More than anything in the world! I long for the day we would all be reunited." More tears begin to flow from her eyes. "We all took heavy losses in what happened during the battles of the Great Betrayal. We lost loved ones, people afterwards grew hate for one another including my kind, and we lost our sister. I felt like it was my fault for what happened to Corin's mother. Nikai and I kept our distances from each other because we got into some foolish arguing about what happened to our sister. Our prides of being right kept us separated for so long. She is the only person I thought of that might be able to help us. Keep Corin protected. That was our sister's one last request of us. Work together." She continuously cries in front of Jo.

Jo grabs a cloth. "Hey Kikai, slow down and use this." She wipes her face. "Magic or no magic, you are doing the right thing. Okay." She starts to smile. "Speaking of families, we better check up on everyone else."

As Jo begins to walk, Kikai grabs him by the wrist and gives him a hug. "Thank you for letting me share my feelings." She kisses him on the check. Jo begins to blush as they walk towards his men. The two of them notice a crowd near the water by the sands. As they run closer to the scene, someone appears washed up on the shore.

One of the Centa people began to use mouth to mouth to breathe life into him. "Oh no the prince! There's no pulse."

Kikai walks through the crowd of soldiers and Centa people. "Please everyone, give me some space. Let me try."

Jo helps clear space for Kikai. "Back up everyone, back up now, let her help."

She looks at Jo. "Jo, give me your helmet please." He hands over his helmet. She walks over to the ocean water and scoops water into the helmet. She kneels next to the passed out young man with the helmet full of water. She closes her eye and breathes while chanting. "Life, life, give me strength to save this life." She opens her eyes as they become brightest blue that is blinding to the eye and her hands dipped in the water light up as blue as her eyes. She drinks the water from the helmet and places each hand on a body part. His head and his heart. Her glow begins to transfer into the young man. After several long minutes, he coughs up water and awakens.

"You did it! You saved our prince!" the Centa people cheered.

Kikai holds the young man's head. "Your alive now."

He opens his eyes and sees his people. He stands up and looks around. "Seena! Seena! Where is she? Oh my god what happened!? I thought I was dead. Where am I?"

Kikai and Jo became startled. Jo helps him up. "How do you know Seena?"

"She's my sister" he said. "My name is Bravera. I am from Centa just like everyone else here. I came here to seek answers in Mt Hiya, find out what happened to our father, clear our people's names to live back on this island."

Kikai responds "Your sister came her two days ago looking for you. She's with my nephew Corin looking for you."

"She and Corin are in great danger!" said Bravera. "I escaped from imprisonment. Some King named Feroick rules Mt Hiya and is in search of the last remaining stones. I overheard his servants and himself gloating about it for nearly weeks. He walks around with black and gold clothing wielding dark magical powers enabling him to control people. He controlled everyone here!"

Kikai grabs Jo by the arm. "This is not good. Not good at all!"

"We must make our way to the Natura Village now!" said Jo. The people of the Sandlands and the people of Centa begin to speak amongst themselves. Some want to venture, while others do not.

Kikai asks Bravera "Can you remember anything else?"

"All I can tell you is that right now at this very moment King Feroick's men are out there in Natura Village and it won't be long until they come here. I must find my sister before this happens."

"Pay attention" said Jo. "I want my best soldiers and the best of the Centa soldiers to come alongside the three of us heading into the Natura village. I want the rest of you to all take the rest of the boats near the docks and head to the Centa islands and get others to aid us."

The Centa people raged outright as they were not fond of the idea. "Hey! We didn't ask for this nor do we want to be part of this."

Bravera quickly interrupts the naysayer. "Enough! You will do as he says. My sister Seena is still out there and if we don't do our part to help find her you will pay by death or by my fist. I am your prince and you will work alongside them. Understood?" The people of Centa immediately stopped fussing and moved towards the request by Jo. "Okay guys, what's next?"

Jo calmly looks at Kikai and then back Bravera "Let's go to Natura Village."

"I cannot avoid the dark magic surrounding the gates Jo. It will hurt me badly" said Kikai.

"Remember that experience I told you about?" Jo winks right at Kikai. The three of them walk over to an old tree with rocks circling it. Jo reveals the tree has a door leading towards steps underground. "Years ago, during my training, my old commander took a lucky few of us with him to build tunnels underground in case we were overwhelmed. This dark magic you speak of isn't not down here. I've had the unique proud pleasure of saving your kind through these tunnels." Everyone followed Jo's lead into the underground path heading towards the Natura Village. He carries a torch to lead the way.

Chapter 11: Battle in the Natura Village

 Corin and Seena sit alongside each other near the broken boulder. They both see Assandie and Nikai arranging the Natura men in preparation for the arrival of unexpected.

"I was just thinking about that fight you got into the days ago. Looks like you get a chance at victory with these invaders coming. I pray however it's not my people." said Seena. "So, how are you doing? I imagine knowing your aunt is a magical being and magic runs through your blood has to be overwhelming news." Seena stands up and faces Corin. She begins practicing her staff movements.

"To be honest Seena, it still hasn't sinked in. Everything is happening so fast and I really don't know what to do. I hope I'm doing everything right." said Corin. "On the bright side, I got my birthday wish in exploring the island. I made friends. Found out I have more family. All I want now is to be alive once this is over with." He smiles about his words and jumps in front Seena playfully. "Good thing you hit me with that staff before it broke. Cause if you did now, I'd be like this boulder scattered on the ground. Tell me something. As strong as a fighter as you are, is it a bad thing that I am coming into this knowing I got my butt kicked by some jerks a few days ago? Cause I can only imagine whatever or whoever is coming right now will be way worse than what I dealt with back home."

Seena spins her staff and plants it to the ground. "Listen, my brother told me long time ago that battles are happening all the time whether we win or lose. Comes down to showing you are not afraid when challenge and adversity arrives." She wipes off the sweat from her forehead of the staff practice. She comes to Corin putting her head on his shoulder in a sign of sincere affection. "I feel bad now for hitting you on your birthday. I will make it up to you somehow. Tell me, what can I do?"

"I'd like for you to find your brother" said Corin.

She puts down her staff. "What about you? Beside seeing the island and all."

"hmmmm" said Corin. "Would you ever want to start a family of your own one day?"

Seena jumps back with her mouth wide open "What!? That is very random." Stunned by his random question, she follows up with a question. "Have you ever talked to a girl before? Beside your aunts?"

"Ummmmmm Wellllll. Nope. You would be the first." Said Corin. He puts his hand back of his head. "Is this a bad thing? Are you gonna hit me with your staff again?" Seena begins to laugh uncontrollably. Her laughter knocks her to the ground. "What so funny?"

She tries to stop the laughing but refuses. "No, I'm not going hit you. Been a long time since I have laughed like that in a long time. You are the first guy to make me laugh. Thank you." Corin takes in the compliment and sees Seena get up to drink water. He enjoys a big blushing smile with a small fist bump quietly. Nikai surprises Corin as he does not notice her until she speaks.

"Didn't know you were so romantic" said Nikai. The two walked away from everyone and sat in the garden. "Whatever happens today, I will make sure you are safe. You the future of our family." She looks over at her husband's tombstone.

"Can I ask you something?" said Corin.

"Ask away" said Nikai.

"Why did you and Kikai have a falling out?" said Corin.

"Going back to the big questions I see" said Nikai. She puts her hands on her hip looking towards the sky. "I really wished my sisters were here. Kikai's way better at this than I am. Last thing I want to do is break his heart about the truth."

"How about I ask you something else?" said Corin.

"Of Course." Nikai in her mind feels the relief of Corin's curiosity going elsewhere.

"If our family has magical powers, how come I haven't seen mine yet? When will I know I can do amazing things like glow green like you do?"

"Well let me see" said Nikai. "The best way I can put it is when the moment arrives. Your grandpa told me that time will come when the moment triggers it."

"The moment? What does that mean?" said Corin

"It means, the moment that will define your character Corin" said Nikai. "My moment happened when I was a child. I saw some boys picking on your mother. My vision turned green and I pushed one of them. He ended flying into a lake." Corin scratches his head and laughs along with her.

"Do funny moments count too?" said Corin.

"I don't see why not. I hope it comes soon for you Corin. Can you make me a promise Corin?" Nikai brushes the dirt off his shoulders. "Promise me you will not change who you are. You remind me a lot of your mother. She was as curious and as innocent as you are now." Nikai pinches his cheek and rubs his head. She starts to walk towards Assandie that is waving at her. "It is time. Corin, go to Mighty. He awaits you inside." Nikai starts walking towards Assandie and the groups of Natura village men awaiting her command. "Assandie, are you and Mighty ready?"

"Nikai, we've been waiting for days like this again. I'm tired of waiting for life to get better. Life before today was not living. It was lying to get by. We want to do, not wait." Assandie pulls out her sword made of dark purple material. "If I must prepare for the worst, then I will have my best."

"Never seen a sword look like this before" said Nikai

"That's because you've never met a lady like me before. Long ago, a time before the Great Betrayal, I sworn to be able to defend my land, people, and myself against anyone. Including those who wield magic powers like yourself. Never thought I'd see the day I'd be fighting alongside magical beings like yourself again outside of Mighty."

The two embraced one another. A high pitch sound can be heard from the sky. It comes landing down towards the feet Nikai and Assandie.

"My Lady, they are approaching in vast numbers but only three are approaching." Lawowl flies back to the sky and flies towards the incoming three men at a safe distance to where Lawowl can speak with them. "You are approaching the sacred lands of the Natura village. As the one of the Sacred Guardians of the island, I must ask you your names and what brings you this way with massive group of people here." As Lawowl speaks to them, his eye color goes from brown to blue indicating his peaceful calm demeanor in speaking with these unknown individuals.

"Sacred Guardian, I am Mustar and this is Kustar. This man we have with us is named Kip. We are in search of sacred stones and a lost child for our King Feroick who rules Mt. Hiya. Kip has told us that what our King searches for lies here. We want to cooperate without violence."

"DON'T LISTEN TO THEM!" Kip screams for his life towards Lawowl.

Mustar swiftly knees him several times to the gut as Kip falls to his knees in agonizing pain. "Quiet or I will do worse to you than what I did to that kid I threw off the cliff." Kip begins to bleed from his mouth. Mustar reveal a bag and throws it towards Lawowl. As the bag lands a ball like object falls out from it. Lawowl looks closer at what the object maybe and his eyes are in shock of the sight.

"That's Hans." said Lawowl.

"Correct Sacred Guardian. Enough of this chatter. Gives us what we came for or everyone in Natura Village will die!" yelled Mustar. Kip looks up to Lawowl as the owl's eye color turns to bright white. Lawowl begins to chant a phrase that immediately turns the sky to summon thunder and lightning.

"Lightning gods, summon the power needed for me to bring justice amongst the hooded ones." Within a matter of seconds, Lightning strikes Lawowl as he screams in pain. The lightning suddenly stops.

 Mustar happily starts to taunt Lawowl. "Those gods never existed Oh Sacred One. It's a false belief."

"Wrong!" Lawowl's feathers light up white as he screams down bolts of lightning from his beak and the tip of his wings right at Mustar and Kustar. The two flew backwards colliding into the groups of mind-controlled people they have assembled. "Kip!" Lawowl screams. "Run now towards the castle. The others await you. I will hold them back while you run. GO!" Lawowl shoots lighting towards the ropes that tie Kip's arms and he begins to run back. "Forgive me my land. I must do this to protect the people and my queen Kikai. You will grow back." Lawowl begins to fly higher up in the air and starts to circle down from the sky. He then flies from one end of the fields of tall grass to the other while striking lightning upon the grass creating a wall of fire in the path of the invaders approaching the Natura village.

Mustar and Kustar slowly begin to get back up. Burnt scars appear on their bodies as well their faces. The two of them shout in pain. "ATTACK!" yelled Kustar. The massive groups begin to run towards the castle. Many of them stop in front of the fire preventing in their path forcing them to move around it. Kustar approaches the fire. "This is good. A chance to show your king how you will serve him." Mustar walks towards the people and without any effort at all, he puts his hand up and yells at them. "For the King." He summons vast winds of air and throws it right at the fire as it immediately disappears. Everyone runs and scream as they approach closer to Kikai and her people.

"Assandie! Mighty!" Kip screams. He runs to them anxiously and enjoys a genuine welcome. "Never thought I'd see you two again! I promise for as long as I'm still breathing and have a head over my shoulders, I will never say stupid things again!" As he catches his breathe, Mighty pats him on the back. "One more thing." He throws a silver necklace at Assandie. "Figured it would help."

She grips it hard and puts it to her chest. She happily pockets it. "Thank you, Kip. "Right now, we have to protect everyone. Especially Corin." Assandie tells Kip to go back where Corin and Seena are. The screams of men become louder as they collide with the Natura men.

"Defend the Land!" Nikai screams. She begins to start pushing off the invaders with her green magic to aid others fighting for the cause. Her sights become set upon the larger crowds seemingly overwhelming her people. She puts her hand up in the air and shouts "May the ground and nature be one with my fight." She slams her hands to the ground and creates an earthquake like movement that shatters the ground. Large brown roots appear from the grown and begin grabbing as many of the enemy as possible slamming them to ground stuck into holes. Lawowl comes screaming back to where the fight is and starts shooting lightning once more at crowds that appear to have circled the castle. Kip, Assandie, and Migty run towards the back area of the castle fighting alongside Seena and Corin. Mighty's punches and kicks were thrown so hard men would fly back or even worse break bones in their body to prevent them from fighting anymore.

"Seena!" Assandie yells. "Time to show me what you got." The two go back to back with one another as they fight off the hordes of them still coming. Assandie cuts through their armor and flawlessly stuns them to ground. "Haha! You like that?"

Seena smirks and turns around at the sight a group of five rushing her. She concentrates on her staff as it glowls blue. She quickly spins her staff as it creates winds to make group twenty yards away from the castle. "That was a breeze" she says as she continues to fight on. One enemy was able sneak past the defenses and rushed towards Seena. He runs as fast as he can with a long spear. "Whack!" She turns around sees that the man has a sword sticking out of his chest. The sword is pulled out and the body falls to the ground revealing it was Corin who saved her. "Thank you Corin."

The man that was stabbed begins to slowly open his mouth. Corin sees him trying to speak. The eyes of the man suddenly closed as he bleeds out from the stab. Corin stares in a state of shock seeing a man die from the swords he used and watches everyone fight for their lives. He looks at his hands as it was his first time seeing someone else's blood before. "What have I done?" he says as falls to the ground in shock.

Kip suddenly turns around and sees Corin on his knees in the crowds fighting each other. "Corin!" he yells. He runs over to him. "Kid, you have to get up now! Please get up!" After a long minute of shock and trauma, he looks up at Kip yelling at him. Suddenly Kip stops yelling and screams in pain as he is stabbed in the leg. He falls on top of Corin and rolls over. He stabs the man who did this to him and looks back at Mighty. "MIGHTY! Get over here and carry Corin out of here Now! Far from here as possible! Don't Worry about us!" Mighty runs over as he effortlessly throws enemies into each other. He kneels towards Kip and prepares to help the stab wound on Kip's leg. Kip immediately grabs him by the hand. "NO! My leg is not important. Corin is most important. Please Mighty." Mighty and Kip stare at one another as Kip sheds a tear and laugh. "I'll be alright big guy. Just take care of the kid." Mighty picks up Corin and starts heading east.

Assandie and Seena continuously fight alongside one another. They that most of the enemy has given up as the guards continue to apprehend them to surrender. They run towards the sight of the injured Kip and help him up.

"Kip, where's Corin and Mighty?" Assandie says.

"They headed east. I told them to get as far away from here as possible" said Kip.

"I see" said Assandie. The three of them head towards the frontlines to see the same result as Nikai and Lawowl along with with the remaining Natura men managed to withstand the waves of enemies. Many of Nikai's vines and roots have appeared to tie down the invaders. Forcing the opposition to give up.

Nikai walks towards the three of them. "Is everyone alright? Where is Corin?" said Nikai.

"Queen Nikai, I told Mighty to carry Corin East from here. Away from this place. For his safety" said Kip. Nikai looks back and sees that Mustar and Kustar have disappeared from the field.

Out of pure instinct, she immediately screams "Lawowl, head east now!". Lawowl flies as fast as possible in that direction. "I hope Lawowl gets there first before those two do." She looks back at Assandie, Kip, and Seena. "Help the other fallen. Don't worry about the enemies, the vines have them tied to the ground right where we can see them."

As Mighty holds Corin over his shoulders running as fast as he can, he suddenly stops at the sight of Mustar and Kustar. "Are you two going somewhere tonight?" said Mustar. Mighty slowly puts down Corin as he begins to wake up. "We are going to make this simple. Let us have the boy and the bluestone. Or we will kill you." Mighty stands his ground close to Corin as he is in front of him. Mustar and kustar both shoot black magical energy towards Mighty's arms holding him. "Looks like we caught a big one" said Mustar. Mighty clenches his fist it glows white countering the dark magic and begins to reverse the tension onto their arms. He throws his arms out causing them to let go as they fly quite far in the air landing hard to the ground.

Corin suddenly awakens afterwards. "Where are we?" said Corin. Mighty points east. "What about the others? We must go back!" Mighty grabs him by the wrist and throws him on his back. Mighty then begins to speak through Corin's mind as he did with Nikai by grabbing him by his hand.

"It wasn't your fault. You saved Seena's life" said Mighty. "There is something I have to tell you. I knew your father personally. Long before you were born."

Corin speaks back to Mighty through his mind. "Wait, how did you know my father and please tell me why you can't talk?"

"Before you were ever born, your father and I were best friends. He saved my life when were children and I told him that I would never leave his side. The day before your father headed into battle of the Great Betrayal, he asked me to look after you in case anything ever happened to him. I did not know you were his son at first, but when I saw the way you acted the day Kip and Assandie spoke, I knew you were his son. You have his heart and your mother's eyes."

Corin becomes overwhelmed at this revelation Mighty has revealed to him. He starts to cry. "Mighty, do you think my parents are really gone?" As Corin awaits Mighty's response, Mighty begins to scream in pain as dark spike hits him in the arm. "MIGHTY!!!"

Mustar and Kustar continuously throw spikes towards Mighty and Corin. "We must serve our King!" said Mustar. The two of them run towards Mighty and Corin. Lightning strikes the two of them in the back.

"Not that Owl again!" said Kustar. "I will take care of that bird. You go after the kid."

Mighty and Corin run further east as Lawowl bought them more time to get away from the hooded ones. As they continue to run despite the pain Mighty is going through with a bleeding arm, Corin hears water. He sees that they have made it to an end of a cliff with a waterfall.

"Well, no more running and hiding you two" said Mustar. Mighty takes a glance at Corin. "Give yourself up. I need to see my family again."

"You took control of those people into fighting all of us. What about their families?" said Corin. "You're a monster." Mighty and Mustar face each other in a standoff two magical beings.

"Okay Mighty, I'm taking that kid!" Mustar aggressively shoots dark magic energy right at Mighty.

Mighty raises his hand to stop the energy. With every bit of energy Mighty has left, he stuck his other hand and grabbed Corin's hand. In a last second effort, he uttered in his mind the words to Corin "Get ready to jump." The wounded Mighty takes on a piece of the dark energy as he moved towards Corin. He grabs Corin and the two of them jump from the edge of the cliff descending towards the waterfall. Mustar tries his best to us his dark magic energy to catch the two falling but Mighty and Corin were out of his range. As they were falling, Mighty tilted his body so he would land first as Corin is safely atop of him. He closes his eyes and hugs him. "Don't worry my young friend. Everything is going to be okay now. You are safe."

Chapter 11: Life Works in Mysterious Ways

Corin eagerly awaits Mr. Stone and Mira's response to his story. "Yeah, and that's how I ended up here." Mira and Stone slowly turn their heads towards one another. Slow levels of laughter turn into uncontrollable laughter as they fall to the floor. "I seem to be really funny these days." He recalls the conversation with Seena in his mind. The two collect themselves and stand up as they begin to whisper amongst each other.

"Well, after hearing your experience of the past few days, me and my wife have something to tell you" said Mr. Stone.

"What would that be?" said Corin.

"We are your grandparents" said Mira.

Corin's face was stunned of many emotions. He looks all around the room. Starts walking around them until he stops in front of them. The mood was of happiness, uncertainty. "Bu HOW!?"

"Nikai and Kikai are our daughters Corin. Carrica was our third daughter. That is the name of your mother Corin" said Mira. She comes up to Corin and puts her hands on his face of joy. "You have your mother's face. Oh, our grandson is finally with us."

"You have your father's bravery as well. Explains how you made it through all of this" said Stone.

'I honestly don't feel brave. More like lucky if you ask me" said Corin. "Now that I know I am safe, please tell me what happened to my parents. I deserve to know."

Stone pats him on the back. "What I've seen in my lifetime, there is no such thing as luck." He stretches after sitting for so long of hearing Corin's long story. "During the fight in Mt.Hiya of the Great Betrayal, your mother went after your father who was fighting the great evils in the Mountain. Mira and I were on the fields defending the lands along with the sacred guardians such as Lawowl."

"You were fighters?" said Corin.

His question cracks a smile on Stones face. "Don't let my old age fool you. I still pack a punch!" He goes on to resume his story. "By the time the fighting was done, we headed towards Mt.Hiya to look for both of them. All we found was blood and bodies. The sight of it was too traumatizing to even continue to aid the Sacred Guardians of the island. Mira and I felt responsible for what happened as we made the mistake of not supporting her love for your father which cost us not just your mother and father but our daughters as well." Stone gets up and puts his hands on his side. Tears start to fall from his face. "If we only supported our daughter's love, we would all still be together." Mira throws a swipe of wind to catch Stone's tears. She places the tear past the window and into the garden outside.

"Don't you see love? Our chance for redemption is here. We are going to make this right" said Mira. She comes over and kisses Stone on the check. She turns to Corin "Corin, hand me your stone?" Corin sticks his hand out with his stone. She magically grabs it and examines it. "This is worth the try."

"what do you mean grandma?" said Corin.

"I mean you are a half-blood of our family. I'm not sure how your magic is going to come out for you, but we will figure it out." Mira comes over to Corin and places her palms on his shoulders. "Were going to do the next best thing first." Mira summons bright light dots to circle around Corin.

"What's going on!?" said Corin. He freaks out at the sight of what's transpiring.

"Give it a moment grandson" said Stone.

After a minute of the bright light dots circling Corin, they chain together to brighten up the room. Once the brightness disappears, Corin appears in a new look of clothes with bright colors of blue and white. "Wow! this is incredible! No more farm clothing!" Corin begins to touch himself all over as he feels joy. He immediately stops and realizes something that came in his mind that he forgot to ask. "Wait a minute. Grandpa when you found me at the waterfall, did you see Mighty?"

Stone comes to Corin and says "I'm afraid not Corin. Did not see a Mighty at all. I'm glad he was able to protect you from Mustar and Kustar." Stone begins to think. "Corin, the one thing that is bothering me about your story is this King Feroick. Why on earth would he want with you and why does he want this bluestone of yours?"

"I'm not sure grandpa. All I know is that he sent them to Natura Village to attack Nikai and went after Kikai in the Sandlands. Their dark magic manipulated innocent people from Centa and even on the island to go after us. Probably even more than we know about. We must find a way to stop him. For my parents. People are depending on us." Corin pounds his fist into his hand. "I hope the others are okay. Everyone for that matter."

"He has vast numbers as you say Corin maybe more. We alone are not enough to take on this dark magic. However." Mira begins to walk back and forth between them. She looks at the bluestone and points at it. "That's our advantage against this King Feroick. His obsession with you and the stone."

Stone asks Mira "I see what you are saying love, but what about Corin? Our daughters?"

"We must find a way back to them grandpa. They would be happy to see you two again" said Corin. "I know I heard it in Nikai's voice how much she misses Kikai."

Stone begins to ramble with doubts. "I wish it were that easy. Failing them as a father hurts more than anything."

"Stop that! Stop it now" said Corin. He raises his voice. His patience has run thin in being a consistent listener to everyone. "Enough is enough. I am tired of this self-loathing and talking of the past. It will only get worse for everyone unless we do something. about some kindness to ourselves and forgiveness?"

"He's right. Our stubborn pride and beliefs have ripped all of us apart." said Mira. Her eyes light up bright yellow. "This is no accident Stone. We have pitted ourselves long enough. We must try. Our grandson and daughters fought together. Broken doesn't mean forgotten." Her eyes begin to fade back to normal.

Stone is moved by Corin and Mira's words. He stands tall while taking a good look at them. "Looks like my fishing days will have to wait." They all share a laugh over his clever humor. The laughing suddenly stops as the sound of knocks on their door occur. "Mira, you expected a visitor today?"

Mira sharply and quietly says "No".

The two of them urge Corin to step back into another room. Stone opens the door. What he sees is absolutely nothing. He looks outside and looks back at Mira. "There is no one out here." Stone feels a thud at his feet. The sounds of the thud were rocks. "HEY!" he becomes irritated as rock bumps into his feet and another to his head. He looks up and sees Lawowl laughing.

"Looks like you haven't changed a bit old friend" said Lawowl. He flies down to the ground. Mira comes running out and the two of them greet and pet Lawowl on the head. "So good to see you two again. I was tracking Corin and Mighty to see if he were still alive for Nikai sakes as well as yours. I suddenly saw and heard a flash of light a few miles away. It brought me here."

Stone picks up a rock and flicks it at Lawowl's head. "You still got the impressively strong forehead you do."

Lawowl shakes his head "You know Stone, I only get one of these."

"Corin, told us everything that happened" said Mira. "What is happening right now? Our daughters okay? Do we have anymore grandchildren that we don't know about?"

Lawowol joyfully fluffs his feathers "Calm down Mira! One question at a time! My goodness!" He stops fluffing his feathers. "Okay, so your daughters are okay. No more grandchildren except the one. Speaking of your grandson, where is he?" Mira points inside the cabin. "May I speak with him?" Mira and Stone nod. Lawowl walks in the cabin and finds Corin. "Wow Corin, you look like a prince!"

Corin chuckles "Yes Lawowl, these clothes are much nicer than the ones before. Grandma gave me a magical touch. Are you alright?"

Lawowl chuckles "Me? Of course! I am sacred guardian. I know you saw me summoning lightning out there. I must ask. If you are here, then where is Mighty?"

"Grandpa Stone said he only found me but not Mighty. Mighty saved my life. All that I can remember was me and him jumping off the cliff as he spoke to me through his mind. Wish I could thank him." said Corin. "I haven't been able to process everything yet. So, my mother is a magical being and my father is human. Tell me Lawowl, why was this a big deal years ago?"

"You have the talent to ask good questions don't you Corin?" said Lawowl. Lawowl hops onto the bed to speak to Corin at eyelevel. "No one was sure how people would take it seeing another form of life loving another form of life. Some supported it while most disagreed. Your mother and father were so good to each other and everyone they strangely scared people. I loved how your father would ask me questions like the ones you ask. People see me as an owl that protects the land but never think to ask about me. Maybe it's my wings instead of arms and legs that I don't earn such conversations. Glad I have this family of yours to talk too. Otherwise, my time would be boring and dull."

"Tell me something Lawowl, why is it so hard for everyone to see each other again?" said Corin.

"Another good question that deserves an even better answer from themselves. What I can tell you is that I have brought this up millions of times between all of them. Believe me I have tried. But eventually they grew quite annoyed by my suggestion that I stopped. I realized it was something they had to figure out. Looks like the solution to everyone is right in front of me." Lawowl pats one of his wings on Corin. "Your courage is stronger than you know. They may not see it, but I do. Come now Corin. We have much more to discuss. I must take you back to Natura Village."

As Lawowl begins to walk out of the cabin, Corin stops him. "Lawowol! Wait!" Lawowl stops and walks back to Corin. "I have a solution."

"A solution?" said Lawowl. "Let's hear it."

"We should take my grandparents with us" said Corin.

"Gasps! Oh, this is going to be good" said Lawowl. He claps his wings and flies up. "You are so unpredicatble. Very well. Let's talk to Mira and Stone." The two of them walk over to Mira and Stone with the idea in mind. Corin explains the purpose.

"We may have a complication" said Stone. "It would take at least a day's walk maybe more depending if there's more of those hooded foes out there. Lawowl would have to make several trips to take us there."

"See what I mean?" said Lawowl. He looks back at Corin laughing. "Oh Stone, thinking so limited is bad for you. You must think a little bigger." Lawowl gives a wink and flies up and away."

"Wise and silly that Lawowl is" said Stone. A gust of wind echoes in the clouds. A large flapping sound from the sky pushes the water and rocks. Lawowl lands in front of them as he appears ten times larger.

"Let us be on our way everyone. A family reunion awaits us!" Everyone hops on to Lawowl's much bigger version of himself. They grab on to his back. He slowly launches into the sky.

"Wow, this is amazing Lawowl!" Corin smiles being in the sky. Mira enjoys watching the joy on Corin's face. Stone is doing his absolute best not to panic. Corin thinks in his mind. "I hope everyone is alright. I hope this idea will work."

Chapter 12: Brothers and Sisters

The day after the battle in the Nature Village…

"Lawowl, please find Corin. Bring him back here safe and sound" said Nikai. Lawowl flies up and begins search the lands east to where he last saw him and Mighty. Nikai walks over to the tallest tree near the castle. As she walks by her people still trying to clean up and recover from the fight, she looks right at the tall tree with two men tied up tightly on the tree. She raises roots and rocks from the ground while forming them into spears. She raises them high and near enough to wear their throats are. "If my nephew isn't found alive, I will take full pleasure of killing you both and feeding your body parts to the wolves." Mustar and Kustar, did not say a word nor did they look as confident previously as they are miserabley beaten. She walks back to her castle to check in with everyone. She sees Assandie and Kip sitting next to one another. "You two have seen better days" said Nikai.

"Thank you Nikai" said Kip. "We owe you are lives." Assandie pats him on the back and puts her head on his shoulder. Kip looks down until Nikai speaks once more. He looks up.

"It is I that should be thanking you. If you did not wonder out nights before and received the letter, we all might be dead. Rather, I would be dead" said Nikai.

One of the last remaining guards runs into the castle calling for Nikai. "Queen Nikai, we have visitors."

"A lady?" said Nikai. She follows the guard outside and sees the sight of her sister Kikai along with Jo and Bravera. The two hold a long stare as they slowly walk towards one another. The two hold hands in a moment of hearts beating and a slow joy to see each other again. Both share a hug that lights up blue and green into the sky as. "Kikai, it's been so many years. I'm sorry for.."

"It's okay Nikai. Thank you for protecting our nephew. For Carrica. I should have reached you more often" said Kikai. The two shed tears as they hold one another in a rare fashion of affection many have not seen from Nikai. Pu-pooh runs towards the two sharing a long hug. "Pu-pooh! You handsome little cub!" Kikai and Nikai hold him up and playfully cradle him like a baby. They set him down and then checks out Jo and Bravera. He proceeds to snuggle on to their legs with his head.

"When he wants affection, he shows it" said Nikai.

Assandie and Kip walk over to see the commotion of Nikai and Kikai enjoying one another. "Never thought she had a soft side to her" said Assandie. Seena approaches the two after helping the guards get back on their feet.

"What's going on over there?" said Seena.

"Looks like a big family reunion over there Seena" said Assandie.

"It's been days and I still haven't seen my brother" said Seena. As she looks on, she two men behind Kikai and Nikai. Her eyes light up and she screams in pure joy "Bravera!" She runs towards her brother. He immediately runs to her and opens his arms for the incoming jump of a hug from Seena. He carries and spins her around. As he sets her down, she immediately punches him in the face. He falls right to the ground. "Don't you ever do anything like this without me again! Mom has been worried sick."

He gets back up slowly seeing her full of anger and love. "I'm sorry Seena. Believe me, after being trapped in Mt Hiya for almost a month, I promise I will never do anything like that again" said Bravera. After he spoke of the words Mt Hiya, Nikai immediately turned her attention to Bravera. She approaches him.

"Mt Hiya? What business did you have up there? No one has been there since the Great Betrayal" said Nikai.

"I came here to this island to find proof that our people from Centa had no part in the deaths of those warriors. We want our homes back on this island again" said Bravera.

"What did you find there and how on earth did you end up finding my sister?" Nikai anxiously awaits Bravera's response.

"I found something worse. I found out many people trapped and caged there myself included. Some king Feroick runs the village there and is obsessed with finding his family along with some sort of stones to be in his possession" said Bravera.

"How did you escape?" said Nikai

"I escaped when I saw an opportunity. One of the guards forgot to close the cage door all the way. I ran for my life. I made it to the forest until the two you have tied up to the tree cornered me at a cliff. Luckily, I survived the fall from the cliff. Mustar pushed me into the water. I thought I was dead until your sister saved me with her water healing magic." Bravera looks to Kikai. "Because of you, I get to see my sister again. Thank you."

"What in the world is that!?" said Jo. He sees a large figure in the sky. He immediately runs up to a nearby stick and hold it. As the figure approaches closer, the wings of Lawowl spread and flap his way down to the ground. He lands near the opposite end of the castle. "Is that a bird?" Jo says. He and the others start walking over. Nikai and Kikai sees Corin coming down from Lawowl's back along with Mira and Stone. Corin runs over to Kikai.

"I never thought I'd see you again!" said Corin. "I've got so much to tell you."

"Looks like you got more than just an adventure" said Kikai. "How about you go catch up with Seena." She looks over at Mira and Stone. "We have some discussion ahead of us." Kikai and Nikai walk over to their parents. The two feel the at one another. Mira and Stone wait for one of them to say the first word. Kikai uncomfortably greets them. "Mother. Father."

"Why didn't you tell us we had a grandson Why hide that from us?" Mira said.

"You suddenly care now after all these years. The last time I checked, you disliked Carrica and Corvan being together. Just like everyone else." said Nikai.

"Carrica was our sister. Your daughter. Your own flesh and blood" said Kikai

Stone felt the urge to yell but looks over at Corin and Seena watching them. "Look. Nikai and Kikai, our first borns, we have made a grave mistake. We paid for it long enough. We lost our daughters affection and even the respect we once held firmly with others. Our grandson helped see through our stubborn pride. Let us make up for it."

"This is going to take some time father" said Nikai. "Part of me is happy to everyone but there are bigger things to address." She points over at Kustar and Mustar. The four of them walk to the sound of insults Mustar is shouting.

"Let us go and the king will let some of you live" said Mustar.

Nikai approaches Mustar. "Oh, you'll be going somewhere." She glows green and picks up the sphere she made previously. She throws it right at the side of his head just piercing the skin as blood appears. Mustar was unphased by her words. His evil snicker surprised everyone.

"He was weak you know" said Mustar. Nikai's glow disappeared as his words clearly affected her.

"I remembered the day he died. Your husband begged for your life to be spared" said Mustar. "It was amusing to me that a human thought he stood a chance. You should of saw his face. Nikai's face was frozen in the moment of listening to his cold-blooded words. "Don't make the same mistake he did." Nikai looked around and saw Kim's face as she is heartbroken for her. She thinks about their moment together at the garden and how her support changed the course of her day. She smiles at her and turns back to Mustar.

"I'm not going to kill you" said Nikai. Mustar is stunned by her decision. The others look on as Nikai steps to the side. She picks up a wooden spear and hands it to Kim. Kim takes a ferociously rams the sphere right into his chest. Mustar screams in pain and agony as the blood gushes out of his body. Nikai walks back to him in his final moments of life he has left. "Your death comes at the hands of human. Rot in hell." As she enjoys the image of him finally dying a miserable death, she looks over at Kustar quietly watching on.

"What about him Nikai?" said Kim. She pulls out the spear from Mustar's chest and aims it right at Kustar's neck.

He looks around and sighs. "Go on. You have every right. What I have done is unforgiveable. I'd like to be with my family again." He anxiously looks between the eyes of Nikai and the spear. His eyes look up at the sun slowly going down and he mutters "We will finally be together again."

"What did you say?" said Nikai.

"I said to my wife and daughter. We will finally be together again" said Kustar. He closes his eyes and thinks of sweet memories he had with his wife. About the time they fell in love and had their daughter together. "I'm ready." As he anticipates the same fate as Mustar, an unlikely person intervenes.

"Wait. Maybe he can help us" said Corin. "Can you help us put an end to all of this?"

"Yes, I can" said Kustar.

Nikai and the others seem unconvinced.

"A matter of seconds ago you were okay with death. Now you reveal to us you can help us. Start making sense" said Nikai. She puts up one finger at the face Kustar. "One chance to explain. Choose your words carefully."

"Understood" said Kustar. "The king requested Mustar and I to help find his missing son and a stone. He is trying to awaken his sleeping wife from a comma. The stone Corin carries is the one he needs the most. He promised us if we were to succeed in helping him get what he wants, he could bring back our dead families." Mira steps in.

"Bring back dead families? That kind of magic no longer exists. It's forbidden" said Mira.

"With respect, I'm afraid your wrong" said Kustar. "He wields the dark forbidden magic you speak of. He can control people to do as he pleases. If he gets a hold of that stone, there's no telling what he can do."

"How do we know this is not a trap for all of us?" said Nikai.

"Because it isn't sister" said Kikai. "Jo and I saw it back in the Sandlands. People who once invaded us were people from Centa. They had no idea where they were under his dark spell" said Kikai. "What Kustar is saying holds truth."

"Agreed. I was prisoner there, they had somewhat of a dark eyed trance to them" said Bravera.

Corin ask Kustar "Am I the son he seeks?"

"I'm not entirely sure. If he is, he is a terrible father. He wants the stone you carry. You may be his son or maybe not." said Kustar. He resumes his attention back at Nikai. "He is not as powerful as he claims. There are moments where the dark magic can overwhelm him. My plan is to take advantage of his ignorance. If Corin comes with me to Mt.Hiya it'll be my best chance to kill him. Make him think I'm giving him what he wants. Corin distracts him long enough for me to come from behind and kill him."

"You will not take our only grandson!" said Stone.

Corin looks around and sees everyone in pure disgust of Kustar's plan. The group is split in both agreeing and disagreeing with the plan. "No, I will do it" said Corin. Everyone began to outrage. "I know this doesn't seem like the best idea, but I have to do it. We cannot allow more families and innocent people out there separated because of him." He grabs the spear Kim holds and stands in front Nikai. "My Moment" he muttered in his mind. "Everyone here has done their part to help. I need to do mine. I have what he is looking for. Please I must go."

After moments of speaking with one another, Kikai comes to him. "Are you sure this is what you want? Honestly."

Corin nods "Yes Kikai. We cannot continue to live like this. I have been saved by everyone here. It's time I do the same."

"You grew up on me too fast" said Kikai. She hugs him. "It took a special kind of thing to happen to bring all of us here." Nikai cuts the rope that holds Kustar to the tree.

"What do you get out of this since you are attempting to kill this king?" said Nikai.

"A chance to tell my wife she was right" said Kustar. "Thank you Nikai."

"Remember what I said. If he is not back alive, that's your life" said Nikai. "For now, we must all eat." Everyone slowly walks back to the castle as Lilly and Kim prepare food for the family and friends. Seena walks up to Corin. "Hey Corin, after dinner can we talk?"

"Of course, Seena" said Corin.

Chapter 13: Leap into the Unexpected

Everyone is now eating the feast thanks to Lilly and Kim's masterful cooking. Dozens of chicken, fruits, bread, and vegetables in Nikai's castle to feed the village and everyone who battled. Kustar sits outside of the dinner festivities next to the garden while others enjoy each other's company.

"Does he not eat or like food at all Nikai?" said Kikai

"I'd feel a bit odd by the situation of eating with the same people he tried to help kill." said Nikai. She continues to eat her food. "Pass the bread!" Mira looks at her.

"Oh Nikai, still eat the same way you did when you were a little girl" said Mira.

Kikai laughs and says "Yeah, I'd be left with only the vegetables." Nikai slowly levitates a fork to Kikai's plate and pulls the chicken leg off. She happily devours Kikai's chicken.

"There's all the vegetables just for you Kikai!" Nikai snickers and looks right at Corin. Corin then sees Nikai attempting to drink her wine. It slowly floats out of the cup and into Kikai's

"I'll drink to that" said Kikai. She winks right at Nikai as the two share laughs at each other's competitive humor in front of everyone. Everyone stops as their father raises his glass.

"A toast. To new beginnings!" Everyone cheers to the toast except Corin. "My grandson, what's wrong?" Corin looks at Stone. He then points and looks at Kustar outside waiting. "Grandson, you barely touched your food."

"I know. I want to give it to Kustar. May I be excused" said Corin. Mira encourages him to get up and go. Everyone watches Corin walk over to Kustar with his plate of food.

"In all my years of life, Corin is something of a sight to see. He breaks bread with the man who almost kills him. I wish Carrica could see what he is becoming" said Kikai.

"What would that be?" said Nikai.

"A leader" said Kikai. Kikai picks up her plates. Nikai tells her to put them down to allow her servants to take them away. "No, it's quite alright. I enjoy doing the dishes."

"Want some company?" said Jo. She smiles to the idea as she grabs his arm. the two grab all the dishes of everyone that is done eating.

"Oh, I see more grandchildren coming your way" said Mira. Stone rolls his eyes. Mira steps out and takes a closer look at Corin speaking with Kustar.

"I figured you could use some food Kustar" said Corin. "How are you doing?"

Kustar takes the food and begins to eat. He continues to look at the stars. "I'm not quite sure Corin. One minute I am chasing you and Mighty off a cliff. The next day your breaking bread with me. Sort of a strange circumstance to comprehend."

"Believe me this isn't what I'm used to neither. I thought I would be stuck in the Sandlands for the rest of my life making food for everyone. Next thing you know I have a mysterious bluestone, met a family I did not know exist, and about to go to a place that makes me scared and nervous all at the same time. My father and mother went there to never return. Never seen them my whole life. I understand you quite well" said Corin. He takes a piece of bread off his plate as they continue to talk.

"I have to admit, I admire your courage to stand up for me knowing I nearly killed you. Young men like yourself don't have that kind of courage" said Kustar. "Wish I could take everything back, but I can't. I will do everything in my power to make this right so others can be with their families again."

Corin asks "Tell me something, what changed your mind to help?" Lawowl watches from a distance by a tree listening to their conversation.

"Honestly, it was the way everyone saw each other with such joy. Joy that I used to have with my own family before I served King Fearrick. I had a little girl that I would spend all the time in the world with. Those days were the best days of my life. Now, before today, I have lived a life of hatred and depression because of how they were killed by a monster of a person while I was out defending my village west from here. I do not want mercy for what I have done, I just want a chance to make things right to see them someday. If making things right means killing that King Fearrick and ridding his dark magic powers, then so be it." Kustar puts his hand on Corin's shoulder. "Listen to me. No matter what happens, I promise to make sure you come back to them in one peace." He looks back at the castle with everyone eating and enjoying one another. "My father once told me this and listen carefully. Never keep a lady waiting." He points at Seena that eagerly looks and waits for Corin at the broken boulder. "Go on Corin I'll be fine. Kustar pats Corin's shoulder twice and resumes looking at the stars.

Corin heads over to Seena. He sits next to her. "Hey, you wanted to talk to me. What's on your mind?"

"My brother and I were talking about everything. Once you set off tonight as we wave you off, we were going to head back home to Centa" said Seena.

He takes a small exhale to himself. "This wasn't what I was hoping she wanted to talk about." Corin comes out of his thoughts and replies to her. "Of course. I understand. You did say you only came here to find your brother." He tries to lighten up the mood "You remember how we saved Jo and you knocked out four of those guys? I bet they woke up the next day with huge headache!"

Seena laughs hysterically. "I never thought about it that way. I will surely miss your sense of humor. I was told by Kip you stabbed a man trying to kill me?"

"Yes, I had too." Corin's butterfly like feelings come back as she stares into her big shiny eyes on him. "I wish could have done more. I have never done anything like this before. I hope this doesn't make me a bad person." She listens to his trembling of words. She happily sits closer to him.

"It was either him or me. You saved my life. I am alive because of you. You're the reason why I got a chance to slap my brother today" said Seena.

He cracks a smile and laughs. "For a guy who taught you how to fight he didn't see that one coming." She laughs along with him.

"He most certainly did not" said Seena. The laughs eventually faded as Seena and Corin continue to look at one another. She smirks as he seems to have trouble coming up with words. "What are you thinking about?" she said.

"Okay, I think your pretty" said Corin. He quickly opens his eyes at her and closes his mouth. He takes his hand off. "Wait! I, um meant to say…" In his thoughts, he starts to panic. "Crap! I think she's going to hit me again!"

She grabs him by the hand and sounds displeased. "Just pretty?"

"Wait wait. Let me think" said Corin. "Okay I got it!" He nervously smiles at her. "Okay, I've never done this before but If you hit me in the head again, I'll understand why."

She smiles at his quirky remark. "I'm not going to hit you." Corin closes his eyes. He leans in and kisses her. "Corin?" "That was my forehead."

He opens his eyes "Sorry I meant too…" Seena grabs him by his face and kisses him back.

"We have another thing in common. You were my first kiss" said Seena.

"Lawowl turns to the sight of them making out. "Oh goodness, just tell her how you oh! Looks like love is in the air tonight." Seena and Corin walk back to the castle holding hands. As they enter, Kikai and Nikai decided to tease Corin as they happily cheered for their nephew once Seena walked away to speak with her brother.

"You've got good taste in girls" said Nikai.

Kikai happily chimed in. "Looks like you guided her into love."

"Stop it you two your making me blush" said Corin.

"Are you blushing Seena?" said Bravera. He laughs at how silent she became. He can tell she is happy and happy to see her smiling after along adventure to find him. "Well whatever it maybe I like this side of you." Seena turns and looks to her brother happily as she drinks in joy.

Bravera puts his drink down. "He's brave. I admire him. But to be honest, I think we should go back."

Seena slaps him and speaks aggressively. "NO! You nearly made it out of there and were gone a month."

Bravera shakes his head and stays calm. "Listen sister, you speak truth except I didn't find any proof of our people's innocence. Please, are father was murdered and I want to know why. If the killer is there, I want to avenge our father." Seena sees the intense look in his eyes while trying to find the words to not upset him.

"Brother, I understand. I just don't want to lose you too." Seena reaches for her brother hands. "Let us see how this goes with Corin first. Maybe he will find the truth without anyone dying."

Bravera raises their arms together and sighs in knowing Seena speaks truth. "Okay, I hope Corin's idea works. But if it is longer than a month, were coming for him." She starts to smile at her brother agreeing with her thought. He throws a little smile at her. "Can't wait to tell mom you have boyfriend now." Seena pulls away from Bravera and blushes.

Time slowly passes by as everyone continues to enjoy one another. As Kustar enters the castle, the joyful laughing slowly stops as everyone sees he is prepared. "Corin, it's time." Everyone walks outside to prepare a sendoff for Lawowl and Corin. "We should return by tomorrow morning."

"Morning? That's quite the time don't you think?" said Mira

"He's right Mira" said Lawowl. "This trip will require myself to use a lot of magic to get us here and back" said Lawowl. "I will make sure we get there safely and back." Lawowl emerges large once again as Kustar and Corin hop on his back.

Before Corin makes it to Lawowl's back, Seena immediately grabs him from behind. "Be careful, comeback to me." The two share a long passionate kiss that moves the hearts of everyone.

Kikai and Nikai at the same time said "Love." The two looked at each other and smiled.

Mira and Stone approach Corin. "Grandson, please take this with you" said Stone.

"What is this Grandpa?" said Corin

"This was your mother's. She wanted you to have it" said Mira. Corin receives a double merged stone made of pink and blue. "This was her good luck charm. She carried it with her everyday including the day she met your father at the same waterfall we found you. We hope it brings you luck as it did her."

"Most importantly grandson, it's one of a kind made of pure genuine love. No dark magic can penetrate it. May it protect you Corin" Grandpa Stone gives his him a hug as well as Mira. The two of them and Seena step back to allow Lawowl prepare to fly. Kustar looks back watching them knowing the importance of what he must do.

"For our families" said Kustar.

Chapter 15: Fearrick's reveal and plea

As they continue their journey through the air to Mt.Hiya, Kustar feels an incredible pain in his head. King Fearrick's voice is heard in his mind. "Kustar, your efforts to take me and my power will not work. Did you really think I would not find out? You belong to me." said Fearick. Kustar screams surprise Lawowl an Corin.

"What's going on Kustar? Who are you talking too?" said Corin.

 Lawowl hears screeches in the air. "Everyone, hold on tight!" Quickly Lawowl notices arrows flying at him. "We must be getting close. Kustar, Corin grab each other. I must drop you both off." Without any hesitation, Kustar and Corin grab one another to prepare for a tough landing. Lawowl spots a part of the mountain with enough room for the two to land upon. He flies low enough to safely drop them there with out any injury. He continues to evade the barrage of arrows.

"You okay Coirn?" said Kustar.

"I'm okay. Where's Lawowl?" said Corin. He looks up and sees bolts of lightning strking the archer's post and the feet of all Fearrick's men. Lawowl hovers a few feet across the entrance of Fearricks temple facing the remaining men lightly throwing their bows to the ground surrendering.

"Enough! As the last of the Sacred Protectors, I ask you to surrender yourself Fearrick. You get one chance" said Lawowl. A servant comes out and walks towards Lawowl. He raises his hands up while waving a white banner meaning surrender to Lawowl's request. Fearrick walks outside of his temple and sspeak to Lawowl from a distance yelling.

"It appears there's a mistake oh sacred protector" said Fearrick. He continues to walk past the archers and guards. "Leave us now!" he screams as they all move back inside the temple. "I'm here for one thing. To have my son and family back. Why do you come here striking lightning upon me? Are you angry about your failures years ago?"

The look on Corin's face felt a powerful shock in hearing Fearrick's words. "Could he be my father?" he said in his head. He turns to Kustar. "Do you know what he is talking about Kustar?" Kustar shakes his head indicating he has no understanding of what Fearrick speaks of.

Fearroick's eyes light up pure black and has Lawowl in a confused state. "You are not the last protector of this island. You were the one who was supposed to protect all of us from doom, but you failed. You are a liar and a disgrace to the people of the island." He continues to stare deep into the eyes of Lawowl. His arms raise out and he challenges Lawowl. He shoots black beams out of his hands and continues to taunt Lawowl. "It your smug confidence that blinds you costing you all the lives of all the protectors of the island. It didn't help you then and won't help you now!" Lawowl's heart begins to race. His eyes begin to shed tears of pain as his memory replays the events of the ones he lost in battles. He is frozen in a moment of suffering that he did not intend to want to remember.

Kustar looks at Lawowl and sees a dark magic flowing around him as Fearrick continues to speak. "We must help him." He and Corin begins to climb towards the edge of the mountain side where Fearrick is. They make it to the entrance of the temple. Kustar turns to Corin in a moment of clarity. "Corin, no matter what happens, I will protect you. Once he shared his final thought with Corin, he turns towards Fearrick. He grabs the nearest throwable rock he could find and throws it at the taunting of Fearrick towards Lawowl. "Whack!" The rock flew in the air and immediately hits Fearrick right on the head as the dark magic he wielded disappears for a moment. Lawowl falls from the sky landing hard on to the bottom of the mountainside. The two begin to fight. Punches, kicks, and magic shots were being thrown at one another. Kustar landed a perfect left hook while Fearrick pulls out a dark dagger and stabs him in the leg.

Kustar falls to the ground, Fearrick immediately pounced on him and picked him up formed a dark dagger and places it his throat.

"Dad!" Corin screams out of desperation. "Please don't kill him."

Stunned by the sound of Corin's voice, Fearrick speaks calmly and is shocked by the sight of Corin "Is that really my son?" he says in his mind. "My son. What on earth are you doing with this Kustar and Lawowl? These are traitors. They are the reason why I was never able to see you. They were all in this together this whole time."

Kustar begins to speak "He is a liar Corin. Don't listen to him."

"Shut up Kustar!" said Corin. He then looks back at Fearrick. "Where is my mother?" The look in Corin's eyes sharpens of courage despite the stressful situation that he has placed himself in. "Let him go. If you are my father, then you will tell me where mother is."

Fearrick throws Kustar to the side. "Take him away. I will deal with him later." his guards carried the wounded Kustar to the cages. He approaches Corin slowly and opens his arms to him. "I'm sorry for everything my son." Corin hugs him in what appears to be joy. He looks over Fearrick's shoulders looking at Kustar being carried away. The two make eye contact with one another as Corin gives Kustar a wink.

In Kustar's mind he says aloud "I don't know what you are doing Corin, but this better work."

Fearrick and Corin enter the temple together. "Father, there's so many questions I must ask you."

"My son, I have all the answers to your questions. I will not let one more moment slip by. For now, we must retire until morning." Servants come to the two and prepare their quarters. The sound of rain is heard outside. Fearrick comes outside later in the night alone and walks over to the edge of the mountain looking upon the island. "Soon, no one will be able stop me and my purpose."

Meanwhile…

"Gasps!" Lawowl awakens from being knocked down from the sky. Rain continues to pour over him. As he continues to blink, he opens his eye to see the world is moving. He turns his head and sees that he is being carried towards a small cabin in the forest. Too weak to move, he tries to speak once he is placed on solid ground. A cover is thrown on him to dry him off. "Where am I?" The one who carried him to the cabin gently combs his head. Lawowl feels the sensation of relaxation throughout his whole body. The hand stops right on the place of his head.

"Lawowl, can you hear me?"

Startled at first, Lawowl replies "Yes, I can hear you. Who are you?"

"I am the one who saved you. I'm also the one who saved another."

Lawowl opens his eyes and gets up feeling completely fine once again. He moves in circles and flies out of the cabin and on to a tree. He speaks aloud to the one in the cabin. "Thank you. Please come out so I can see your face." The person who spoke to Lawowl comes out of the cabin. It is a familiar figure as Lawowl is stunned by who he is seeing before his very eyes. "Impossible. How can this be?"

The person waves at Lawowl to come from the tree and. Lawowl gladly flies down and lands softly onto the person's arm. "There isn't much time. Find the blue light Lawowl. Fly back. They need you."

"What about you? I cannot leave you here all by yourself. It's too dangerous and he is beyond powerful even for you to handle." Lawowl is immediately petted once again.

"Alone yes. But together, victory is on the rise. Go my friend, you will find the blue light sooner than you know. Time is of the essence." The hidden identity launches him into the sky as Lawowl flies away from Mt.Hiya in search of the blue light.

Chapter 16: The Shining Truth

The following day back in Natura's village, Seena and Bravera are walking away from Nikai's castle right before the sun rises. "I wonder if any of them saw us leaving?" said Seena. "Would have been nice to have said bye before we left brother."

"Don't think like that Seena. Think positive. We will return and say those byes later. Right now, it's about us finding justice for our family. Our people." Bravera walks with worry understanding how hard it was for him being trapped at Mt Hiya for a month. He and Seena both stop walking. "I'm sorry about my emotions last night. I don't mean to come off as stubborn. I'm sorry I got you into this mess. This is my fault."

Seena looks at him realizing he feels responsible. "Listen to your own advice. This is not the time to think like that brother. In a strange way, I have to thank you."

Bravera's confused by her remark. "What? Why on earth would you be thanking me? I'm the whole reason why you came to this island and I put you in danger."

"This has been the most exciting thing I've ever done! I got to be in combat, made new friends, met a magical being that fixed my staff, and even found love." Seena begins to kick rocks as she thinks of Corin days prior kicking rocks. "I really slept on it well last night about justice brother. If I were willingly able to risk my life to come here for you, then I can do the same for our people. Our father."

He starts to resume walking as well as she. "I really like the sound of that word you just said."

Seena smiles and laughs "I said a bunch of words Bravera. Which one is it?"

"New. That is something all of us need right now. Everyone on this island as well as our people always talk about the past. They talk about it so much that we cannot even enjoy living in the now. I'm glad me and you are doing this."

"Father would be proud of us. You almost sound just like him." Seena pushes him on the shoulder as he pushes her right back. The two stop and look back as they hear running footsteps heading towards them. "Assandie and Kip?"

"Told you it was them Kip!" said Assandie. Kip and Assandie take a moment to catch their breathe. "Hey, we couldn't stay there much longer either. Was it cause they all talk too much and argue so quickly?"

"No, Assandie it wasn't that. Me and my brother are heading to Mt Hiya. We have unfinished business there. It involves our father." Seena looks towards Kip. "How are you holding up Kip?"

"I'm better now Seena. As Nikai's guards, we must make sure that kid Corin is okay. He is a brave one for putting his own life at risk for the sake of everyone else. But I am not convinced on this plan. Might be a trap or they're in trouble." Everyone else agreed at Kip's statement. The walking resumed as the four of them begin heading towards Mt.Hiya. Bravera notices a bright blue light emerging from Seena's staff.

"Sister what's happening to your staff? Is this the magic you speak of?"

"Yes, brother it is but I've never seen it light up without my hands on it before." Seena pulls it out and holds it admiring its gaze. "I wish Mighty were here." Kip and Assandie both sigh into deep thought missing their massive figure of a friend.

"There it is! The blue light!" Lawowl hoots in excitement as he flies down for a closer look at the light. "What a most wonderful surprise!" Lawowl lands closer to everyone as he greets everyone. "Hello again everyone!" The whole group says hello at the same time.

"Lawowl are you alright? where's Corin and Kustar?" said Seena

"Nope! But to be honest, I did not know if I were going to make it back here" said Lawowl. He starts fluffing his feathers. "I'm alive which is all that matters. Right now, Corin and Kustar are in Mt.Hiya as we speak. They're in trouble."

"I knew it Assandie" said Kip.

"What exactly happened Lawowl?" said Bravera.

"This King Feroick nearly killed me. I remember seeing Kustar fighting him as Corin was on the side watching it. Next thing I know I wake up being carried to a cabin in the forest and being restored back to full strength. The one who saved me told me to find the blue light which this appears to be your staff Seena." He flies up into the air and becomes a giant version of himself to carry everyone on his back. "There's no more time to wait. Get on!" In a matter of minutes, Lawowl and the others arrive to the cabin where he was rescued. As Lawowl allows everyone to hop off his back, he looks around looking for his savior. "Hello?" He starts to hoot and hop on different tree branches looking around. Bravera and Seena look around the cabin.

Kip and Assandie sit on top of a log. "Never thought I was going to fly in the air today. Did you Kip?"

He starts to chuckle. "You know what Assandie, at this point everything lately has been a surprise. One day we try catching Corin and Seena to turn them into Queen Nikai for a reward. Next thing you know we no longer want the rewards and want to be guards. Life is full of surprises." His shoulder begins to get rubbed. "Wow Seena, thank you. That feels quite nice."

Seena is looking down at her hands. "What are you talking about Kip? My hands are in front of me" said Assandie. The two turn to look at one another and slowly turn around. They scream at the top of their lungs.

"MMMMIIIGGHHHTTTYYY!" screamed Seena. She runs over to the three of them hugging and joins in. Lawowl flies over to the scene.

"I made sure not to tell them it was you. Surprises are the best!" He flies over to Mighty's arm waiting for him to land and communicate. "So mighty, what's the next step."

Mighty points to Mt.Hiya and puts his other hand on Lawowl's head. "We are going there now. Must save Corin. I have a promise to keep."

Lawowl tells everyone else the plan. Kip, Assandie, and Seena begin asking questions to Mighty but he simply put his hand up and pointed to the mountain. "He said He will explain everything for another time. Right now, we must save Corin before it's too late." He flies off Mighty's arm and prepares for everyone to hop on his back. Suddenly, Lawowl turns his head to Mighty. "I mean no offense, but I'm not sure If I can carry you."

Mighty snickers. He whistles and claps towards some bushes. A small creature appears.

"Pu-pooh!" said Seena

Pu-pooh happily comes to Mighty as he magically rubs his back. After a few short moments of rubbing, Pu-pooh turns himself into a much larger version of himself as a wolf big enough to carry Mighty over to the Mt Hiya. Mighty hops on and waves off Lawowl as he takes off. Two ladies approach Mighty from the side as they put their hands on his back.

"Good Luck Mighty" said Kikai.

"Yes, bring our nephew back home" said Nikai.

"I will make sure he comes back. He is the future." Mighty rides off with Pu-pooh deeper into the forest heading towards Mt.Hiya.

Meanwhile back a top of Mt.Hiya…

Corin and Fearrick are at a long table with many foods to choose from fruit, bread, meat. "Son, why aren't you eating?"

He looks around to see many empty seats as it brings a disturbing chill through his shoulders. "Father, I'm sorry. Not quite hungry just yet."

Fearrick continues to eat and then raises his finger while drinking wine. "Oh well. You said you had questions. Well, now's the time to ask." He puts his hands down out of Corin's sight as they begin to have dark air come out towards Corin's direction.

"Why do you live here and not with our family back in Natura or Sandlands?" said Corin.

"Well for one, that is not my family. That was your mother's family. They despised me because I was not a magical being like themselves. They were not as accepting to our love for one another. Glad to see they could accept my son." Feroick smiles cheerfully when he points to Corin. "Do you have another question for me son?"

"How come you never visit? No one really knew what happened to you or mother" said Corin. "Grandma and Grandpa presumed you to be dead."

Fearrick gets up and snaps his fingers commanding one of his servants to bring his robe. He walks over to an empty seat next to Corin. "Oh, I've tried many of times and every time I came to find you, they told me to try again another day. Overtime son, I stopped mainly to tend to my duties as king and as hero. Big responsibilities in making sure our island is protected."

"King and a hero?" said Corin.

"Yes, I'm not sure what they have told you but I'm the hero who stopped the madness in the Great Betrayal years ago. With my own bare hands, I stopped the hooded ones and their dark magic. The people here have claimed me as their King which makes you heir to the throne son."

"Father I was told that you weren't alone in stopping them. There were other great warriors here. Do you know what happened to them?" Fearrick's confidence slowly changes as he walks away with an apple in his hand. He comes back to Corin and takes a bite.

"Son, I'm afraid through victory still came defeat. All of them were killed in the end. I tried to save all of them, but it was too late. Breaks my heart just thinking about it." Fearrick takes another bite of the apple. "They weren't just warriors but my friends. Brothers and sisters." Sniffing and huffing came from Fearrick. He reaches for a cloth to wipe his face. "Sorry son. I felt horrible about what happened. I tried reaching out to their families, but they were full of hate and disgust with me. A lot of them threatened to kill me if I ever set foot at their villages again. That hate grew like wildfire. It spread throughout all of the villages and they separated from one another."

"So that's why there are rules to not set foot into other parts of the island. I hated those stupid rules" said Corin. He sees a sudden smile from Fearrick. "Why are you smiling?"

"I'm smiling because that's exactly how I feel. The apple does not fall to far from the tree. In here son, no one can tell you anything. You have all the power to do as you please." Fearrick throws away the apple and puts his hand on Corin's disturbed shoulders. Dark magic begins to emerge from his hand on to Corin's shoulders. "Stay with me my son. You, your mother, and I can be together once again."

He feels cold air on his shoulders and hears whispers in his ear. "Be one of us" the whispers say aloud. Corin quickly grabs the stone his grandma and grandpa gave him. A shining beam of light suddenly appears on his shoulders and blinds Fearrick. "Father! Are you alright?"

"Yes, I'm alright son. Must have been the food that has got me blinking in the eyes" said Fearrick.

"My mother, where is she father?" said Corin.

"I will take you too her son." Fearrick and Corin begin walking through a hallway past the king's throne. They both stop at a door. Fearrick turns to Corin. "Son, are you ready for this?"

Corin breathes heavy at the words. He nods and says "Yes, I'm ready for this." Fearrick opens the door. The two see a glowing light of his mother in a glowing crystal. He runs up too her as she is in a deep sleep. "Mother! What is happening to her?"

"She's in a deep magical comma. I've been trying to figure out how to set her free from this crystal for a long time." Fearrick walks over to the side of the crystal. "I've tried everything up until I saw this." He pointed at a spot of the crystal. "A special bluestone is the key setting your mother free. I lost it years ago. I've looked all over the place for it."

Corin's eyes lit up at the thought of Kikai's gift. He pulls it out of his pocket and shows it to Fearrick. "This is it."

"Yesssss! Hand it to me my son so we can set your mother free!" Fearrick reaches for the stone but Corin pulls it away from him. "My son. What are you doing?" He tries to be cool and calm as he sees Corin is holding the bluestone he has longed for.

"I have one more question for you. Possibly the easiest question of your life" said Corin. He sees Fearrick clenching his teeth and tightening his fists.

Fearrick puts his head down and then slowly raises it. "Okay son, I'll answer one more question. But after that, we free your mother."

"Couldn't agree more father" said Corin. "Tell me father. Do you remember the day you first mother?"

Fearrick smiles trying to hide his frustration at Corin. "It was a bright and sunny day it was. I saw her watching the ocean in this beautiful white dress. I was nervous to speak to her. But thanks to your uncle, he encouraged me to come to her. We walked through the forest and picked flowers together. I later told her my love for her at the same beach I saw her and we both fell in love. We then had you." Fearrick claps his hand and looks up. "Soon we will be able to tell you more Corin. Would you ever so kindly hand me the stone my son?"

Corin looks at the stone in his hand. He reflects on his journey up until this point. He thinks of Mira, Stone, Kikai, Nikai, Seena, Kip, Mighty, Assandie, Mighty, Pu-pooh, and Lawowl. He smiles back at Fearrick awaiting him to handover the stone to set his mother free. He looks at Fearrick. "Fearrick, a king and a hero, for all of what you have done for me and the people of this island."

"Thank you, my son. The waiting is making is driving me silly. Son, you are making me nervous" said Fearrick.

"It wasn't the Sandlands Fearrick" said Corin. Fearrick realizes that Corin caught him in his lies. "It was at a waterfall where you and mother first met." Corin puts back the stone in his pocket and steps back to look harder at the guilty Fearrick. "You are not my father! Who are you!?"

Fearrick laughs hysterically at Corin. He points at his mother. "She was supposed to be mine. My wife." Then he points at Corin. "You were supposed to be my son! Instead she picked that disgusting thing called my brother." Feroick throws off his robe and glows dark bright yellow. "I'm your uncle. Your dear old uncle Fearrick."

"You killed those people. You killed the great warriors. You mind controlled people with dark magic to tend to your needs and separate them from their families. You separated me from my own family." Corin becomes furious. "WHY DID YOU DO ALL OF THIS!?"

Fearrick continues to laugh at Corin. "Foolish boy. If I were a cold-blooded killer, I would have already done so with you. I simply gave these people a choice. They refused. Refusing me is disobeying me which is something I will not tolerate in my kingdom."

"This is not your kingdom. You are the one who betrayed your own friends and family for selfish needs. You are the reason why no one trust anyone on this island anymore. People have suffered as you sit here in on Mt.Hiya laughing at everyone." Corin's eyes looks right at Fearrick as he is the one who responsible for the Great Betrayal.

"Oh, young Corin. You look just like your father right after I pushed him off that cliff outside. It is a shame really it is. That he is not here to defend his little boy. You know you can still be my little boy if you hand me that stone."

Sickened by his words, Corin fires back at him with words of his own. "My father was a brave man. One that you could never imagine of being. You coward. You would push him off the cliff from behind cause If you were face to face with him in real combat, you would lose."

Fearrick's eye lightened up and smiles back at Corin. "Ohhh so there is fight to the cooking boy of the Sandlands. Tell me something. Does that mean you will face me in real combat Half-Breed? Here, let me show you HOW!" Fearrick runs towards Corin and takes a swing at him with his dark magic. Both Corin and Fearrick immeadiatley fly back crashing into opposite walls of the room. "Impossible!? How did you do that? I have the most powerful dark magic on the island." Fearrick sees Corin is glowing of all different colors.

"My son." Corin hears a voice full of peace and love. "Is that you mother? What's happening to me?"

"Yes, Corin. It is your mother. "Your moment has arrived. You triggered the stone to give you the magical powers that's been waiting for you. This is your time son." said Carrica.

Corin asks her as he stares Fearrick laying on the ground helplessly. "What must I do mother?"

"Listen to your heart. Your heart is the key my son" said Carrica.

"Okay mother." Corin walks over to Fearrick. He stands above him seeing that Fearrick continues to laugh.

"Go on boy. Do what your father could not. Kill me" said Fearrick.

Corin raises his handout with the stone. He closes his eyes and remembers the man he stabbed to save Seena's life. "Honor" he says aloud. The magical colors that glow from Corin quickly float to Fearrick and start to tie him up.

"What's happening to me?" said Fearrick.

"What should have happened a long time ago. Stopping your madness." Corin raises his hand as Fearrick's body becomes frozen still. He grips his hand as it squeezes all the Dark Magic in him and the temple starts to shake. The shaking stops. Corin opens his eye and sees the temple has changed. The brighter colors begin to fly throughout and bring life into the colors of the temple. "Who was that mother?"

"That was your father, Corin" said Carrica. "His spirit has been with you this whole time."

Corin looks towards his mother in the crystal. He goes to the side of the crystal where the stone must be placed. He reaches his pocket for the bluestone. He inserts it into the slot shaped as the stone. The Crystal glows and magically begins to disappear as his mother falls from the crystal landing into Corin's arms. "Mother!" he speaks to her and sits her down.

She awakens gaspsing for air. "Oh my, where am I?" said Carrica.

"You are in Mt.Hiya Mother" said Corin.

"Corin! My son" said Carrica. She puts her hand on his face. "You've grown so big now! Look just like your father."

Corin helps Carrica up to her feet. From a distance, voices where heard all over from the temple. Loud running footsteps approached the two.

"Corin! Are you here!?" said Seena. She sees the sight of Corin and his mother Carrica. She runs to him hugging and kissing. "I was worried about you. Are you alright?"

"Yes, Seena I'm fine" said Corin. His mother admires Seena's strong affection. "This is my mother Carrica" She blushes at the the sight in seeing Corin's mother.

"It's an honor to meet you. I'm Seena" said Seena.

"I can see your quite fond of my son" said Carrica.

"C'mon everyone. Everyone else is out there." Seena leads the way into the main hall room where the others have found all the cages broken, servants throwing away robes, and running out of the temple. Kip, Assandie, and Mighty come running up to Corin.

"Oh my god! Everyone is here! Mighty how did you?" said Corin.

"Long story kid" said Kip. "Where's this Fearrick?"

Corin points in the direction of where he is. They come back with Fearrick tied up and over Mighty's shoulder.

Lawowl flies over to them. He quickly tells them all. "Come outside now! Look!" Everyone follows Lawowl outside to the entrance of the temple. The dark magic that once flowed through the temple has disappeared. Another sight that they see is the rest of the island no longer has dark magic floating around. He turns to Corin. "Corin! You have done it! Our people can walk freely once again! The hooded ones are no more!" Cheers can be heard throughout all parts of the island. Everyone at Mt Hiya applauded Corin as he stands with his mother and Seena all smiles.

"Wait! What about him?" said Corin. "He must answer for the crime and suffering he put everyone through Lawowl."

Lawowl flies over and uses his claws to pick Fearrick off Mighty's shoulders. "Don't worry Corin. I will take care of this." Lawowl flies off into the sky. Everyone afterwards all marched down the mountain safely.

"Mother are you okay to walk?" said Corin.

"Oh yes my son. Your father always said to keep moving forward." Carrica wraps her arms around Corin as she is finally happy to be with her son.

Chapter 17: A Hopeful Island

One month later…

Corin returns to the Sandlands in a much different role. No longer is it just him and Kikai making the food for the village, but it is now an entire group effort by all who live there. Jo and his son are making sure everyone contributes. Kikai sits next to Corin on a log near the shore. "I have to say I'm quite happy with your birthday wish."

"Here you go Kikai. Fresh bread" said Mikke.

"Thank you" said Kikai.

Mikke turns to Corin and offer him some bread. "Hey, I have something for you Mikke."

"Really? for me" said Mikke.

"Okay close your eyes" said Corin. He closes his eyes and suddenly falls to his knees. Corin strikes Mikke right in the gut. "Sorry, I owed you that." Mikke holds his stomach painfully as he walks away back to his duties that Corin once did.

"Have a lot more confidence I see" said Kikai.

"No Kikai. I have always had it. It was just a matter of me going out to find it" Corin grins right at Kikai as he refers to the wish of seeing more of the island on his birthday. Shade from above comes down upon Corin. Lawowl hoots and lands softly in front of Corin. Kikai walks back to her home to join Carrica and Seena.

"Oh Corin, the island feels like it once did. So happy to just fly around! It was all because of you." said Lawowl.

"I'd like to think we all did it" said Corin.

"No no no! Young Corin." Lawowl flies up and flicks his wing at Corin's head. "Enjoy this feeling. You deserve it. In fact, I believe you deserve to be King!"

"A king? Why?" said Corin.

"Because out of the decades that I have existed on this island, you clearly are the most different of all people. You brought your own family back together, solved the mystery of the Great Betrayal, and made different people work together for one common cause. Your most fit to be the king and leader. I cannot wait for the rest of the island to meet you. I've already helped passed the message to others."

Corin scratches his head and throws a rock into the ocean. "I'm not sure how to feel about this idea. Do you think it be okay if I took some time to think about this?

Lawowl laughs "You truly are unique. It keeps me guessing what you will do next. Of course, you get time to think it over. But remember, that time to decide will be coming sooner than you think."

"Thank you Lawowl. Can I ask you something?" said Corin.

"Yes, you may my king!" Lawowl chuckles "Just giving it a try"

Corin smirks "Now I know how Nikai feels. It's about what happened at Mt.Hiya. Minutes before you all arrived, my stone glowed and my mother spoke to me spiritually telling me my father emerged in beams of light and helped defeat Fearrick. Could it be possible that he is still alive just as I have found my mother?"

 Lawowl is stunned by his reveal. "I cannot answer that properly. Not until I do some investigating of my own through others around the island that may know this better than I. For now, Corin, let us keep this between us until I discover more now that the dark magic is no longer."

Corin hugs Lawowl. "Agreed Lawowl. I will do my part as well."

"Will continue this another day. Today, enjoy being with your family. I will keep a lookout on things my future king." Lawowl gives a wink and flies in the sky back to the Natura village.

Carrica and Seena watches the two of them speak. "So Seena, have you told him yet?"

Seena coughs up the wine shes drinking. "What?"

Carrica laughs "You haven't told him yet? That I'm going to be a…"

"Stop! You stop right there" Seena cleans herself up. "I will tell him soon I promise."

Carrica smiles as she puts her hand on Seena's stomach. "I know you will. I look forward to meeting the rest of your family Seena. Speaking of, how is your brother?"

"He's doing well Carrica. Pretty soon everyone from Centa will be here and we will have our original homeland back." Corin and Kikai join the two. They all walk into Kikai's new home and enjoy their company amongst each other.

Meanwhile in the Natura village Nikai and Lawowl are seen helping build more homes for everyone. Kip, Mighty, and Assandie are on guard making sure everyone is behaving and cooperating with Nikai's plans.

"This is such a thoughtful idea Nikai" said Lawowl. "You may not like being called queen of this village but have the qualities of one."

"After the night we all fought, I did some thinking and I have to continue to build relationships with everyone" said Nikai. "Make sure we have the village looking more together again. Making homes and even planting seeds for gardens." Nikai uses her powers to help the ground rise. "Maybe even have little hills so the little ones can play." Lawowl and her laugh at the kids running up and down the hills as they fall. "By the way, exactly what did you do with that Fearrick?"

"I put him right where he belongs. Isn't that right Mighty?" The two of them look over at Mighty as he nods his head with a big smile. He points at a Stoned crafted cage filled with green armored magic that is impossible to break. "We are going to keep him alive as our way of making peace and communications with the other tribes. Soon we will reach out to them to make our island beautiful again like it once was before this Great Betrayal."

"Good idea Lawowl" said Nikai. "We shall call this the great rebirth!" Kustar approaches Nikai. Nikai turns to acknowledge him. "Kustar, what brings you back here?"

"I decided to pay everyone a visit. I figured that would be okay. Seeing that Corin is safe and this Fearrick is imprisoned." Nikai looks back at Lawowl and the others as they approve of Kustar's presence.

"You came through for us. You have been redeemed and you are a friend now." said Nikai

"Thank you Nikai. May I lend a hand here? Said Kustar

"Why interested Kustar? It is a fresh start for everyone. You don't owe us anything" said Nikai.

"I know this" said Kustar. "However, I'm seeking a new purpose. Months ago, I was promised that monster over there I would be able to see my family again even after death. Now that I know the dark magic is no more and the promise was false, I figured my family would smile over me knowing I am not in pain no more. I'd love to help other families be back with their loved ones no matter how long it takes."

"Give him to us Nikai" said Kip. "We could use the help in covering more ground in reaching out to other villages. More people the better." Assandie and Mighty agree alongside Kip.

"Alright Kustar. Welcome to the Natura Village" said Nikai. Everyone around applauds her announcement.

"Very good Carrica" said Stone. Stone and Mira appeared carrying a wagon full of fresh fish and other foods. "I finally got a chance to fish!" Everyone laughs. "Hope all of you are hungry." Stone walks over to Kustar. "This time you sit with all of us okay." Kustar and Stone handshake one another.

"Well done Nikai well done!" Lawowl flies up in the air gliding around watching everyone the entire island as he moves in circles in the sky. He hears familiar sounds of others in the sky. A wolf that howls, A lion that roars, and birds screaming from other parts of the island. "The Others! Oh, I cannot wait to see them all again soon." Lawowl responds to the others across the island as beams of light begin to shoot across the island signifying unity once again. "Hope has finally returned to the island."

www.ingramcontent.com/pod-product-compliance
Lightning Source LLC
Chambersburg PA
CBHW031349060726
47590CB00007B/2693